AF427887

All Snakes Don't Hiss 2

Bestselling Author O'Sharra

Copyright © 2022 O'SHARRA
Published by T'Ann Marie Presents, LLC
All rights reserved. No part of this book may be reproduced in any form
without written consent of the publisher, except brief quotes used in reviews.
This is a work of fiction. Any references or similarities to actual
events, real people, living or dead, or to real locals are intended to
give the novel a sense of reality. Any similarity in other names,
characters, places, and incidents are entirely coincidental.

"Sometimes you have to cut off your finger, just to save your hand."
-Future

Chapter One

CAMI

2016

I need a one dance, need a Hennessy in my hands.

Drake's hit song "One Dance" pumped feverishly throughout the college frat party as I bounced my ass on a random stranger. I was sweaty, high, and as drunk as a backsliding alcoholic as the guy I was dancing with rubbed his hands all over my body and tried to slide his fingers up my short skirt. I swatted his hands away and continued to twerk as my feet slid to the front of my open toe heel sandals. Catching the hint for a few minutes, he put his hands on my hips and began to grind his dick on my butt. The cloth separating us was better than him trying to finger fuck me on the dance floor, so I continued to enjoy myself. Besides, I had a lot to celebrate. When the song switched and the DJ mixed in R. Kelly's reggae song, "Slow Wind", the upbeat vibe changed into a lazy slow wind as all the Philly girls in the club began to do their best dutty whine. That was all the greenlight the creep I was dancing with needed as his hands moved from my sides and began to creep up my skirt. When his entire palm cupped my pussy through my panties, I jumped away from him quickly.

"You perverted piece of shit!" I screamed at him as I turned around and slapped him across the face.

"Bitch, didn't nobody tell you to wear that little ass skirt; it's barely covering your ass. Then you want to complain when a nigga try to touch on it," the tall sexy dreadhead complained as he walked closer to my face. The same rugged appeal that had once turned me on and made me want to flirt with him, now intimidated me as he towered over me.

"Back the fuck up," I replied aggressively. "What the fuck are you going to do if I don't?" he questioned while putting his hand around my throat. I was surrounded by people, and not one person said anything while I was getting assaulted. The DJ hadn't even cut the music. Everyone was too busy dancing and in their own world to try to step in and help me.

"You doing too much," I told him as I attempted to back away. Knowing that he was in control, he pulled me back closer to him. "No, I'm not doing enough." He began to squeeze tighter around my throat with one hand while using the other to put his hand back up my skirt. He began to rub roughly on my pussy lips.

"We going to have some fun tonight," he whispered in my ear while licking his lips. I weakly struggled to push back from him as the rank smell of alcohol seeped through his pores.

"It don't look like she want you to be all over her like that," I heard a familiar voice shout over the music from behind me. "This my bitch, and you in our business. We do this every night; she's just acting like she doesn't like it," the boy lied as he continued to sexually assault me. In that moment, the full gravity of the situation hit me. I was a recent high school graduate, on a college campus that I didn't even plan to attend in the fall, and I was alone. My best friend, Glow, had gotten her period and decided that she didn't feel up to coming out to party with me tonight. Instead of staying in with her, I was determined to go out and celebrate that I had graduated at the top of my class and gotten accepted into my first choice college.

Now here I was, after a few blunts, a few shots, adrenaline pumping, and at the mercy of some drunk creep, who didn't understand what no meant.

"I said, back up off her!" the boy yelled again to my attacker.

When he was ignored, he stepped from behind me and punched the nigga in his face, causing him to release me and fall on his drunk ass.

"This didn't have nothing to do with your bitch ass." The boy sprang to his feet and charged at the nigga who had just stood up for me.

When they began to fight, the same people who were ignoring me being damn near molested on the dance floor, were now taking notice, whipping out their phones to record and laughing as my attacker got his ass whooped.

"Cut the music. What the fuck is going on over here?" a dark-skinned, muscled boy with a buzz haircut approached with two flunkies behind him. The DJ silenced the music, and all eyes were on the situation unfolding.

"Break this shit up," he told them as they snatched the boys apart.

"SEAN?!" I screamed out in surprise when the boys were untangled and was able to make out the identity of the person who had stood up for me.

"This nigga jumped in my business while I was trying to get some ass to take to the squad tonight," the boy who I had just been dancing with yelled angrily as the two boys held him back.

"Well, the nigga you're referring to is my little cousin. Apologize to him and get the fuck out of here, rapist," the buff boy told my attacker as his two flunkies and Sean looked at him.

"My - my bad, Legend. I didn't know that was your folks. My bad, lil' bro," the asshole apologized to Sean.

"It wasn't me you was out here trying to rape. Apologize to my friend, Cami," Sean told him aggressively while walking in his face.

"My bad. Put on some clothes if you don't want that kind of attention," the rapist replied with the backhanded apology while getting the hell out of the frat house.

"Get your little friend out of here, cuz. She looks young, and you can't beat up every drunk nigga who tries her. He was the first thirsty creep, but he won't be the last one tonight. College niggas be on high school girls like white on rice," Sean's older cousin spat.

"Put the music back on." He raised his red cup to signal the DJ, who began to play the music again. He and his two flunkies walked to the opposite side of the party, leaving me and Sean alone.

I was mortified that I had been called out as just "a high school girl", and my best friend's boyfriend had to have my back in a room full of people who were willing to let me get raped and passed around.

"Thanks, Sean." I stormed away angrily and headed towards my car to get the fuck out of there. His older cousin had all but threatened that this shit was going to happen again, and I wasn't with it, so I was out.

"Wait, Cami!" Sean ran behind me, following me out of the door. The cool breeze hit my face, causing some of the sweat to dry. I knew I was being irresponsible by heading to my car to drive home after I had been drinking and smoking, but Cheyney University's campus wasn't too far from my house. Plus, my mother was pulling a late shift tonight, so she wouldn't be home to chew my head off about the dangers of drinking and driving.

Turning around, I crossed my arms over my chest and stuck one foot out. The air was causing my nipples to stick straight out through the thin fabric of my crop top.

"I already said thank you. I'll make sure to tell your girlfriend that you rescued her drunk best friend from possibly getting raped. My hard headed ass just had to come to the party without her," I retorted.

"I didn't come out here to judge you, ma; that wasn't your fault. These college niggas prey on high school girls and college freshman. I've been to enough of my cousin's parties to know what goes down. The shit ain't right, but it's the reality of all colleges. Instead of blaming the boys, they blame young girls and tell them to be more careful and travel in packs," he told me sincerely.

"Are you good? Can you make it home?" he asked.

"I'm ok. I can take care of myself, but thank you. Glow really has a good guy. Another nigga probably wouldn't have said shit," I chortled.

"Well honestly," he cut me off and stepped closer to me.

"I didn't do that for Glow; I did that for *you*." I had always caught Sean's lingering eye, and he always laughed a little too loud at my jokes. I chalked it up to it being all in my head, but he was confirming what I had already known.

"Well, Glow is my best friend, so you did it for her and not me," I snapped on his ass while walking away and getting in my car.

"Well, I'm still following you home to make sure you make it safely." He ignored me and walked to his car, which was parked a few cars down from mine.

Not in the mood to argue with him, I let him follow me home. When we made it to my house, I parked in the driveway and instead of pulling off like I expected him to, he pulled into my mother's spot directly next to mine. I rolled my eyes in annoyance.

"Sean, I'm good. You wanted to make sure I'm home, and as you can see, I'm home." I put both arms in the air and waved them around. I didn't understand why all the men around me were acting hard of hearing tonight.

"Well, I drank a little too much, and I wanted to see if I could come inside and have a glass of water. I only need to sit down for a few minutes. You want to rush a nigga away like I didn't just do you a favor," he reminded me while shaking his head.

Smacking my teeth, I shook my head and went over to the front door. Sean had hung at my house a few times, but the difference between then and now was that he was around Glow. He and I had never been inside of my house, or anywhere for that matter, alone.

A part of me felt that it was a little shady, but I dismissed those feelings as paranoia. I had known Sean for years, and he and my best friend had been in a relationship since sophomore year. I knew where his parents lived and everything about him. I was safe with him.

Letting him inside of the house, I pointed to the couch, and he went over and sat. I went into the kitchen, made him a large glass of ice water, and brought it to him as he used the remote and turned on the power to the TV.

"I'm going to lay down, so just shut the door behind you when you feel rested enough," I told him nonchalantly as I walked to my bedroom. Shutting the door behind me, I went to my adjoining bathroom and began to undress. I threw my clothes in the hamper and grabbed shampoo so that I could wash the smoke out of my hair. A few minutes into a scalding hot shower, I cried as the water ran down my face and washed the tears down the drain. I had almost lost my virginity to a drunk at a frat party. There was no doubt in my mind that the guy would have raped me if it weren't for Sean. I would be forever indebted to him for stepping in and saving me from a careless mistake that could have gotten me fucked up. I prayed and thanked God for showing up right on time as I scrubbed my body, my hair, and the memories of the night away.

After a relaxing shower, I wrapped one towel around my hair, one towel around my body, and proceeded back to my bedroom to find something to sleep in.

"NIGGA!" I screamed out in surprise as I jumped back and gripped the towel tighter. Sean was laying across my bed comfortably, flipping through the channels. He was shirtless, showing off his chiseled arms, muscular stomach, and broad shoulders. He had gained his amazing physique from playing left fielder on our school's baseball team for the past four years.

He laughed at me lazily, and I couldn't help getting lost in his smile.

"Relax, baby, it was lonely in that living room. I came back here to keep you company," he flirted.

"Look, you are my best friend's man, Sean. Nothing about this situation is cool. I did you a favor and let you chill. You rescued me from the bullshit situation back there. Don't get it twisted. You are not about to be a player and bounce between friends," I put him in his place as I walked over to my chest of drawers to grab my cute pajama set. I had always found it weird that Sean had chosen Glow over me. I was thicker and prettier than her. I chalked it up to him knowing that he wasn't heavy enough to fuck with a bitch like me.

I had niggas from every grade chasing me around Maynard High School on the south side of Philadelphia. Every athlete, nerd, and nobody wanted to get between my thighs, and that was just at our high school. On the outside, I had the boys my age as well as the men my daddy's age wanting to be a sugar daddy to take care of my young ass. I wasn't fucking or dating; it only made them try harder to get at me.

I dropped my towel at my feet, exposing my naked body, even though Sean was only a few short feet away. I loved to tease niggas knowing that they wouldn't get anywhere with me. Even though Glow had let Sean pop her cherry our freshman year, I was saving my virginity for someone special. I couldn't wait to go off to college and meet one of those fine, paid ass New York niggas and let him be my first everything and become his spoiled wife.

His sharp breath let me know that he appreciated what I was showing him.

"Cami, me and Glow haven't been happy for a long time. The only reason I haven't broken up with your girl is because I know I was her first, and I don't want to hurt her feelings," he told me as he stood from the bed and walked over to me.

"If I'm being honest," he began as he grabbed underneath my chin and lifted my face up so that I could look at him in the eyes, "It's always been you that I had feelings for. Glow was just a cheap replacement because I felt that I could never have you," he admitted bashfully while looking away from me.

I smiled shyly.

"Yeah, ok. You just spitting some game. You handsome and all, but I'm not Giovanni. It's going to take more than being fine and popular to get between my legs," I shut him down, while reaching for my coochie cutting boy shorts and matching tank.

"I'm more than just a handsome face, baby. I just got a full ride scholarship to Texas A&M University to play baseball, and after I get my degree in Psychology, I'm going to join the league and play baseball professionally. Did you know that baseball players are the highest paid athletes? Not basketball or football. I'm going where the money is, and I want you to be mine," he begged.

"Nah, I couldn't do that to Glow. That girl loves you," I shook my head at him.

"Fuck Glow. It's you I want. I'm going to break up with her ass as soon as I leave for school." He caressed the side of my face, causing my nipples to harden.

He reached for the towel that was holding my hair and released my long, red tresses. My hair fell down to my waist as I stood in front of him shirtless, barefoot, and only wearing my boy shorts.

Pulling me closer to him, he leaned down and whispered in my ear, "I'm in love with you. Be mine. Let me make love to you, Cami." His voice caused the hairs on the nape of my neck to rise. I began to breathe harder as he caressed my shoulders.

He leaned down to kiss me softly but still with enough strength to let me know that he was in control of the situation. I had lost all common sense as he rubbed all over my body.

He smelled so amazing. He was so enticing, his chocolate skin was flawless and as smooth as a Hershey's bar.

To hell with Glow, I thought to myself as he pulled my boy shorts down, picked me up, and placed my legs around his shoulders.

What was supposed to be a one time thing, ended up lasting the entire summer. I hated lying to Glow and sneaking behind her back, but I was hooked on Sean. When it was finally time for us to part ways, he went to Texas, and I went to New York. The move to New York was as short lived as the fling, because a few months later, I found out I was pregnant.

Returning home with a large belly and shattered dreams, I blamed the baby on a made up guy and enrolled in community college with Glow. I realized that this baby was my karma for stabbing my best friend in the back, so I blocked Sean and moved on with my life as if he never existed. Maybe in some twisted way, he did genuinely love me because he never stopped trying to reach out to me, even after I changed my number a million times.

Chapter Two

CAMI

PRESENT DAY

As we drove from Rhode Island back to Philly, I had decided that Bak was right. I wasn't going to beat a dead horse with a stick. I had made some fucked up mistakes in my past, but karma had already done worse to me than Glow ever could. Every time I looked at my son, I was humbled and reminded of where I wanted to be versus where I was. If Glow didn't want to be my friend, I was a grown ass woman, and my life would continue. There were other women who would hang out with me. Me and Qyleek's wife, Raleigh, had hit it off from the first time our men set us up on a lunch date. She was more aligned with what I wanted my future to look like. She was a wife, mother, and businesswoman. I texted Raleigh the great news of my engagement and set up a play date for the boys and a lunch date with her for tomorrow.

When we finally made it to my mother's house, Princeton must have been watching us through the window, because he ran outside with the speed of lightning. He was acting like me and Bakari had been gone for three months instead of three days.

"Mommy, Mommy, I want some cereal!" Princeton tugged at my leg, looking like his father's twin. I couldn't help but to see Sean's face when Prince smiled at me.

"Don't try to go behind my back and get that crap from your mother just because I wouldn't give it to you. That is not a real breakfast, so you won't be eating it around me," my mother told him as she walked out the door behind him with his backpack in her hand.

Before she had the opportunity to say another word, I stuck my hand out in front of her, and she began to scream dramatically and jump up and down.

My mother had never been married or even proposed to, so I could tell that she was genuinely excited that I was breaking the curse of just being another man's baby's mother and not his wife. She ran over to Bakari and hugged him tightly, rocking from side to side. He laughed as he hugged her back. "I told you I would make an honest woman out of her. You don't have to worry about your baby girl or your two grandchildren not having what they need or not being taken care of as long as I got breath in my body," he told her sincerely. I could tell that he meant what he was saying. Bakari was a real one, and I was truly blessed to have him.

"I know, son. Welcome to the family. My daughter is lucky to have you," she replied, taking the thoughts from my mind.

"Ok, little one. You've run your grandma ragged. Let your daddy put you in the car. I need to talk to your mother about something," my mother told Princeton as she got down to his level. He put his arms around her neck and hugged her tightly.

"I enjoyed you, grandma, and Mr. Davis is so much fun; he let me have ice cream late and—"

"Ok, that's enough. Carry your little ass to the car." My mother silenced Prince before he spilled any more tea. Knowing his grandmother's sense of humor, Prince laughed loudly as he released his grandmother and ran over to Bakari.

"Hold up, young lady, you have some explaining to do. How did the man from the church go from sneaky link to regular house guest?" I asked her while crossing my arms over my chest and sticking my hip out.

"I don't know how many times I have to tell your ass that I'm the mother, and you're the daughter…with your little nosey butt. Now get in here," my mother retorted while pulling me by the hand and leading me into her two story home.

Walking in behind me and closing the door, her face dropped from playful concern to genuine worry.

"Oh, my God, baby, have you heard about what happened to Giovanni?" my mother asked me urgently.

"I haven't talked to her since we had a words a few days ago," I replied nonchalantly while shrugging my shoulders.

"Well, she needs you now, Cam. She's in jail for trafficking a whole U-Haul truck full of drugs. It's all over the news, and everybody's talking about it," my mother told me urgently. My heart dropped. There was no way my straight-laced best friend could have been trafficking drugs. Her ass was scared to walk across the street when the light wasn't red because jaywalking was against the law. She was the type of person who would drive miles down the road to find a side street to turn on just to avoid making a U-turn.

"Ain't no way in the hell," I cursed as I reached for my cell phone and attempted to dial her number. I then remembered that the call would go straight to voicemail because she had me blocked. Turning to Google instead, I typed her name into the search bar, and the news articles popped up. The article showed the flipped over U-Haul that I'd just been riding in with her three days ago.

I felt sick to my stomach as I ran to the nearest bathroom and threw up the amazing breakfast that the chef had prepared for me and Bakari before we checked out of the luxury suite. My mother rubbed my back as I hugged the porcelain bowl, praying for it to be over.

When I was finally done, my mom handed me a sleeve of

Saltine crackers and a bottle of water for me to wash my mouth out.

"So, what do you think about this Glow situation? Do you think she was really out here drug trafficking? Are you going down to the jail to visit her and get her a lawyer?" My mother rambled off questions back to back as she wrung her hands nervously.

"Relax, ma, and take a deep breath," I coaxed her.

After inhaling and exhaling, she looked at me intensely to see how I was receiving the news she had given me. She knew that for my entire life, Glow had been the only sister I ever had. She was expecting me to collapse, scream, cry, and kick like a child. That was the reason she had pulled me away from my fiancé; she didn't want me to come undone in front of him.

"Glow is a big girl, mommy. Whatever she has gotten herself into, I pray she gets out of it," I replied coldly.

"Me and her had a huge fight, and we are no longer friends. I've decided to be around women who are more aligned with my future than my past. Me and her have outgrown each other," I told her while taking a bite out of the Saltine cracker.

"Thanks for keeping Prince for me." I hugged her and left out of the door before she had the chance to say anything else. I was a wreck on the inside. I had known Glow forever, and there was no way that she was trafficking drugs, and I didn't know about it. Something fishy was going on, and I could smell it from a mile away.

When I made it back to the car, Princeton was in the back seat, playing with his toys while Bakari was doing something on his phone. When I was safely inside, he pulled off in the direction of our house. After a few minutes of silence, I spoke.

"How did you know where to come and get me from when Glow and I had that argument at the store? I never told you where

I was going," I asked him nonchalantly as I pretended to clean something out of my nails.

"Don't ask questions you really don't want the answer to, wife," he replied before turning the music up loudly.

Chapter Three

Glow

As I lay shivering on the cold cot, I cried but my tear ducts were dry. No longer was there water coming from my eyes because I had been crying nonstop since I was put in the backseat of the patrol car. I hadn't looked in a mirror since I'd been booked into the detention center three days ago, but I felt the bandages on my face, and I was sure I looked a hideous mess. I hoped that the police had gotten me confused and at any moment, the correctional officers would barge into the crowded holding cell and say, "Giovanni Henderson, come with us. We realized there was a mix up and you're free to go." That moment never came. On the second day there, I was told to dress out of my clothes and put on the hideous jumpsuit and sent upstairs, where the female offenders were housed. When they showed me to my cell, a ratty looking white girl with stringy hair sat on the top bunk. She gave me a stank look then turned back to her Bible. When the metal doors clanked loudly behind me, my heart fell to my feet. I was really in jail, and this shit was really happening. I began to hyperventilate while trying to catch my breath. My head began to feel light, and I felt like I was gasping for air. When my cellmate jumped from the top bunk, she grabbed me by my shoulders and led me to the bottom bunk.

"Breathe, mami, just breathe," she coached. Still struggling against myself, she forced my head down between my legs, and my vision went from blurry to clear. She was skinny, but the bitch was strong as she held my head below my waist.

When my breathing returned to normal, I slapped her hand from my back and sat up quickly as my chest heaved up and down. I looked at her, and my eyes began to fill with tears.

"No." She snatched me by my arm and shook me roughly.

"Not in here," she warned like a mother, talking to her unruly child. Gathering my strength, I took a long inhale and exhaled as I quickly wiped the tears from my eyes.

Turning my arm loose, she stood from my bunk and went back to hers at the top. When it was time for us to leave our cell a few hours later, I declined.

"Suit yourself," the guard grinned like a Cheshire cat and slammed the door.

For the rest of the night, I prayed for God to give me strength. When I was too tired to keep my eyes open, I passed out from sheer exhaustion.

The next day when I opened my eyes, I was reminded where I was. Gritting my teeth, I sat upright and placed my feet firmly on the cold floor.

"Morning, sleepy head. My name is Rose," the cellmate greeted me casually.

"Thanks for yesterday, Rose; I've never been through anything like this before. It's a little hard to process it all," I thanked her.

"Word of advice: don't ever say those words again. These bitches in here are like wild animals, and if they sense that they can run over you, they're going to drag your ass. I've been in and out of the system my whole life; I know how this shit works. Either you're gonna fuck or fight, and whichever you choose, you'll be doing it for however long you're here, so choose wisely," she schooled me.

"I appreciate the advice, but this shit is some type of fucked up mistake. When I get in touch with my boyfriend, he's going to get me the fuck out of this hell hole. I don't have to play these little jail games with these bottoms of the barrel rejects," I told her confidently. Sure, she'd helped me out yesterday, but the minute I got my phone call, I was going to call Shovi and get the hell out of this jacked up situation, so she could save her jail survival tips for her next bunkmate.

"Suit yourself," she chortled like she knew something I didn't.

When the correctional officers came around to open our cell, I couldn't deny another meal. I hadn't eaten in days, and I felt like I was about to faint because I was so hungry. Plus, I needed to talk to a correctional officer about seeing if I could get a phone call.

When I shuffled from my cell into general population, I saw women of all shapes, sizes, and colors. I had never seen so many bitches in one place in my life. As soon as we were released from our confines, Rose went over to a group of women and began to laugh and chat with them like they were family.

This bitch is so institutionalized, she thinks this shit is cute. No wonder she's trying to get me acclimated to this lifestyle, I thought to myself. Minding my business, I walked over to the guard and attempted to have a conversation with her when suddenly I felt a shove from behind.

When I turned around, there was a big, butch-looking bitch, grinning at me all crazy.

"Excuse me, slim thick," she flirted while licking her lips at me.

"Don't start that shit, Frita," the correctional officer told her, stepping in to defend me.

I didn't say anything; I just mugged the bitch to let her know this wasn't that.

"I wasn't looking where I was going, CO Brooks, that's all," Frita lied to the guard while still wearing the slick smirk on her face.

"Yeah, ok. I don't give a damn what CO Lee allows on her shift. I'm not going for the dumb shit or risking my job for you. No funny business on my shift. I already have a headache, and I don't have time for your foolishness," the correctional officer checked her.

Frita walked away, laughing and unfazed about what the correctional officer said. My heart told me that I hadn't seen the last of Frita. I knew that the correctional officers couldn't protect me forever.

Walking up to CO Brooks, I began to talk to her.

"Thank you for that," I began.

"Just doing my job, move along, inmate," she answered rudely.

"I didn't get my phone call yesterday, and I was just wondering if I could talk to someone about getting it," I attempted to explain before she cut me off.

"I said move along, INMATE," she spat disrespectfully. Spit flew from her lips and landed in my face, and I felt as low as bird shit on a car window. Rolling my eyes, I walked away from her and headed to the chow hall. Thankfully, I didn't have any issues while eating my food; even though I caught a few stares.

Not having a sense of time really made it fly by and before I knew it, another day was gone. When the guards opened the gate for us to come out for the last time before lights out, shit went left.

Since the day had gone smoothly for me following the incident with Frita, I foolishly let my guard down and walked out of my cell behind Rose, who had run over to her little friends like she did every time they opened the bars. A few minutes after I stepped out, I felt the hardest punch I had ever felt in my life. The punch caught me off guard, and I immediately fell sideways onto the concrete. I could hear ringing in the ear I had been hit in, and the entire side of my face felt like it was on fire. Out of nowhere, I felt multiple feet stomping me in my head, shoulders, and face, and all I could do was curl up in the fetal position as blows rained down on my body from different directions.

"HEY! Break this shit up!" the correctional officers yelled as the women scattered in different directions, leaving me shaking on the ground. That was the last thing I remembered before I lost consciousness.

When I woke up, I was surrounded by white lights, and my head felt like someone had taken a sledgehammer and beat me with it. I tried to sit up quickly, and the dizziness caused me to fall back on the twin bed.

"Whoa, slow down. You have a concussion, dear. You can't sit up too fast," the nurse told me as she rushed to my side.

Tears immediately filled my eyes when I remembered what had happened. So, every day I was in here, I would have to keep my head on a swivel, out of fear that someone would try to hurt me for no reason at all. I didn't understand how the hell people chose to live their lives like this. This was the reason I had gone out of my way to follow the law and be a good girl. I didn't deserve this shit, and I was truly innocent of what they were saying I did.

I broke down into body-racking sobs, as I covered my swollen face with my hands. I felt completely helpless and concluded that death would be better than this. I would rather kill myself than to live my life under these circumstances.

"Hey, listen to me. Listen," the nurse told me, moving my hands from my face. "I can see you have never been through this before, so listen to me. Find some friends and some people to have your back. This ain't the place for you to stay to yourself. There're bitches in here who are passing through and others who are never going to see the outside again. They have nothing to lose, and you have to stand up for yourself," she scolded. "Now take this." She reached in her smock and pulled out a cell phone while looking around to see if anybody was coming.

"CO Brooks told me you didn't get your phone call, so I'm

going to let you use my phone to call who you need to call. Make it quick," she warned as she walked over to the door to look out of it.

Reaching for the phone quickly, I dialed Shovi's number.

"What up, who this?" he answered on the first ring. I could hear laughter and music in his background, but I was so happy to hear a familiar voice, I couldn't even be angry. My heart leapt from my chest with joy.

"Babe. Babe, it's me, Glow. I need you to get me the hell out of here and quick. These bitches jumped on me and —" I began before he cut me off.

"Look, babe, I'ma see what I can do to help you out. Just stay strong, though," he told me, sounding like a fake ass Hallmark card.

"Who is that on the phone, babe?" a woman asked in the background, causing my blood to boil.

"Who the hell is that, Shovi?" I questioned him angrily, sitting up fully, even though my head was pounding, and the nurse had advised me to take it easy. I couldn't believe this nigga was hugged up in another bitch's face while I was going through the worst shit I had even been through in my life.

The girl laughed loudly and shrilly, wanting to be sure that her presence was known.

"Look, just call me back tomorrow. I'm going to take care of everything," he replied before ending the call in my face, causing my heart to drop.

When the nurse walked over to get her phone, I begged her for one more call.

"Ok, just hurry," she urged, walking back over to the door to keep watch again.

This time, I called my mother. After talking to her, I felt a renewed sense of strength. God couldn't be everywhere at once, so he created mothers. My mother assured me that I could get through this the same way I had gotten through everything else ever placed in my path. She had already come down to the jail, contacted a lawyer for me, and put money on my books so that I could make commissary for the things I needed. She had done all that in the four days I had been here. Meanwhile, Cami called herself a best friend, and I hadn't heard anything from her since our fight, even though I was sure she knew what was going on. I began to question if she really ever was my friend, or if I was just somebody there to pass the time.

I found myself thinking of Zay. Something had to have happened to him, because he would've been here for me; he was always there for me when I needed him.

Handing the nurse back her phone, I waited for an officer to escort me to the store so I could buy the things I needed as well as some snacks.

When I was released from medical, I took my purchases back to my cell and made a weapon out of what I had. They'd caught me down bad the first time, but those bitches would have to kill me the next time because I wasn't going down without a fight. My mom had always taught me that if there were a gang of bitches, all you needed was to focus on one. Whatever the group did to you, you would do it to her. Like Rose had told me, the attacks would only get more vicious the more I let them do what the hell they wanted to me. I had to survive.

Later that night, I laid in the cold cot, staring at the ceiling. I missed my iPhone, my flat screen TV, and most of all, my man. Being here in the darkness forced me to think about everything that had transpired over the past few weeks.

I wondered what Shovi was doing and if he was missing me as well.

"He didn't sound too torn up. The nigga at the bar, having a drink and shit," I told myself out loud as I rolled my eyes in aggravation.

Suddenly, I remembered that before I was arrested, I was driving home from the furniture store, and I called Shovi. He was doing the exact same thing — sitting at the bar with loud music, and he'd rushed me off the phone both times. My mind began to replay the events over the past few weeks, and the last time Shovi hadn't rushed me off the phone, was when he was convincing me to take the drive to the furniture store alone because he had to take care of something at his store.

"I tried to get his hardheaded ass to reschedule, now look at me," I said aloud as I put my hands over my eyes in despair.

"Who you down there talking to?" Rose asked, more in annoyance than genuine concern.

"Nobody. I mean, I'm not talking to nobody; I'm just thinking out loud," I replied.

"Word of advice, if you have a man, don't worry about what he's out there doing and who he's doing it with. These men are about as loyal as a sheet of paper flying in the wind. One minute they're so in love with you, and the next minute, they're all up in the next woman's face," she spat.

"No, not Shovi. He's not like that," I defended my man.

She may have been right about jail house politics, but she couldn't tell me shit about the nigga I had been lying next to every night. Although I'd heard a woman's voice in the background, I knew there had to be a perfectly good explanation for it. I wasn't about to let her trash him in my presence.

"What makes him so different from any other nigga?" she questioned.

"Well, he owns multiple businesses. My baby is successful, not one of these leech dudes who want to drop a woman off at work in her car, while he plays video games at her house all day. He has his own house, cars, no kids, and no drama. He's perfect," I bragged. "Plus, he's not the selfish type. You know how women say don't just get a man with money, get a man who's generous with his money? Well, that's Shovi. My baby bought furniture for his stores and turned around and let me run up the tab for some furniture for my apartment as well. He's connected and respected."

"Oh, shit. It's giving big dick energy. You might be right about him. What type of business is he in?" she questioned to be nosey.

"If you must know," I began, "he owns Weed Hut. He and his business partners have multiple dispensaries throughout Philly that legally sell marijuana in edibles and various other forms," I smiled.

"Sounds to me like he's not that generous. You were just earning your keep," she humbled me.

"You are in here for trafficking weed, right? Well, if it wasn't for you, he wouldn't have the weed to supply his stores. Now you're in here, and I'm assuming he's out there because the news didn't say you were with anyone when you got into the accident in the U-Haul. This the type of shit I be talking about. This man has you out here working for him, and he's rewarding you with material shit to make it seem like you're spoiled when in reality, you're just another employee he's fucking," she laughed.

"Niggas ain't shit; that's why I like pussy. Good night, Cellie," she told me before I heard loud rustling, signaling that she was turning over. The cots were so thin, any movement you made sounded as if it were big and dramatic. A few seconds later, she was snoring softly. I stared at the ceiling as her words registered. Taking off my rose-colored glasses, I began to really reflect on what had been going on the past few weeks. Initially, Shovi never gave me the time of day. He always acted too good for me, and the day at dinner, he couldn't wait to tell me how disgusted he was with me for sucking Bakari's dick. Never once had he shown interest — until he suddenly called.

I then thought back to Zay's warning and our argument.

"Well, whatever it is, you need to end that shit because he

isn't the man you think he is," he warned me.

"I overheard him saying that you wanted to be like Cami, and if he made you think that he'd be in a relationship with you, you'd be desperate to do anything." he persisted.

"I'm a big girl. I can make decisions for myself," I said aloud as the tears filled my eyes. That was what I'd told Zay when he tried to warn me about Shovi. He didn't care about me. He never gave a fuck. He knew how much I liked him, and he used that shit against me to get me to be his drug mule. I had been so naïve. Look where it had gotten me. In a cage, surrounded by animals with nothing to lose, constantly looking over my shoulder, while he was out doing the same thing he'd been doing when I called him both times.

The truth hit me in the face like jumping into a cold swimming pool after walking around in the sun for hours. I covered my mouth in shock as the weight of my situation settled around me. I had been the one to sign for the U-Haul truck when he came up with a fake ass excuse for why he couldn't make it. When I received the truck, it was empty. While I was out furniture shopping, the sale associates were loading up furniture and drugs into the truck so I could take them back to Philly. The furniture was just a front because there was no way I would willingly go up to a drug lord and let him load pounds of drugs into a car I was driving. I would, however, transport some furniture from one state to another.

The tears rolled down the side of my face as my heart caved in. Had Cami known what was in the truck? I was so upset about her and Sean that I left her at the store with him. Was it a part of the plan for me to take the fall for this shit alone? Bakari acted strangely when I went to get Cami to convince her to ride with me because he had to have known that I was going to pick up the drugs. Of course, he had known. He and Shovi were best friends and business partners. But did Cami know? Did my best friend allow me to walk blindly into a trap that had just cost me my freedom and everything I'd worked for? The bed squeaked as I turned over face first and buried my face in the thin fabric they called a pillow.

"I care about you, and I don't want you to end up hurt." Zay's voice replayed over and over in my mind. I held the pillow and cried until my head felt like it would explode.

"I need you, Zay. I'm sorry I didn't listen before, but I need you. You're the only person who can get me out of this shit," I cried. I wasn't sure where the hell he was, but I hoped that he could hear me.

Chapter Four

Ta'Shovi

"Didn't I tell you to keep your big ass mouth quiet, Raleigh?" I questioned my sneaky link and the wife of one of my best friends. She giggled playfully, even though I didn't find shit funny. I had promised myself that I was done with her ass, but I still managed to fall back into the pussy.

"Who was that? Your little jailbird? Her ass is all over the news," Raleigh shrugged her shoulders. We were sitting in a secluded booth in the back of Callahan Sports Bar on the outskirts of Philly. We couldn't be spotted together, but I wanted to get a drink before we went to my house for a nasty, sexual escapade. I knew it was risky being in public with her, but I needed some fresh air to clear my head and at the moment, she was the only person available.

My right-hand man, Bakari, had been out of town for days with his woman. Raleigh's husband and my best friend, Qyleek, was on a witch hunt, looking for a nigga he would never find. He would be gone until tomorrow night. He was wasting his time looking for Zay, my other best friend and former business partner, who I had gotten killed because he found out about my illicit affair with Qyleek' s wife. I thought I was rid of him, but Zay was still tormenting my ass from the grave. Qyleek had gone on a dummy mission to Dubai because I placed a resort brochure on top of Zay's papers inside of his desk. I wished Qyleek would move on and focus on more important things, like his wife and kids. If he would dick her down at home, the bitch would probably stop blowing up my phone like an addict. Sneaking around aside, being out with Raleigh was a welcomed distraction from what really had me nervous as hell. I was praying that Glow wouldn't snitch on me for setting her up to traffic my weed across state lines. I had a hundred drivers do the same run for years, but the minute that bitch did it, I lost a hundred thousand dollars' worth of product. I still had to pay for that shit, whether I received it or not. Pissed was an understatement for the way a nigga was feeling. Judging by the phone call she had just made, she still hadn't realized that I was the nigga who'd set her up. She wasn't a fool, though; the light bulb would go off eventually. Luckily, I covered my own ass and persuaded her to put everything in her name. By the time she'd finally have her moment of clarity and try to snitch on me, it would be her word against mine. Her name was on the U-Haul truck reservation and the furniture store order. There was literally no way that any of this shit traced back to me. Still, I had a sinking feeling in my stomach that I wasn't going to be able to pin everything on her that easily.

After a few more drinks, I was ready to head back to my spot and get it cracking with Raleigh. No matter how hard I tried, I couldn't stay away from her toxic ass. I looked over at her, and there were still remnants of a sneaky smirk on her face. I knew a piece of her was happy that Glow was in jail. The past few weeks before the trafficking incident, I had been spending time with Glow in our fake relationship to get her to fall in love and trust me. That meant less time with Raleigh, and even though she was married with children; she was jealous that another woman was taking what would usually be her time.

"Don't speak on shit you don't know about, ma. Besides, have you checked on your husband today?" I taunted her. I could be petty right with her ass if that was what she wanted.

"As a matter of fact, I have. My husband is running around Dubai, looking up camels' asses, and searching in the desert for Zay, the nigga you killed right here in Philly," she smirked before taking a long sip of her dirty Martini. "The things we do for the people we love," she shook her head.

"Don't get it twisted. I didn't off my nigga out of love for your ass. Qyleek would hate the ground I walked on if he found out I was fucking with you. My day one flipping on me for pussy wouldn't be good for business," I told her as I swirled my Bourbon and took a long sip.

"And yet, you continue to fuck his wife," she licked her lips sexually, causing my dick to harden. I had to give her credit; she could suck a nigga's soul from his dick. This freak bitch had even tried to lick my asshole once. Nothing was off limits with her. The last time I fucked her, I had the audacity to bend her over my dead friend's office desk. The friend I had killed because of her ass. The icing on the cake was the fact that her husband, Qyleek, was in the room next door. He could have walked in on us at any time. I knew then that I'd hit a new low.

"Ok, that's enough of the cute shit. Finish that drink and follow me to the spot," I retorted, because for once, I didn't have a comeback. I was willing to kill to cover up this secret instead of just finding some pussy that didn't belong to another man.

Forty-five minutes later, I pounded Raleigh mercilessly from behind while she screamed my name loudly. Pushing the center of her back down to deepen her arch, I plowed into her, almost throwing my hip out. Suddenly, my phone blared out loudly, knocking my focus. Taking a deep breath and wiping the sweat from my forehead with the back of my hand, I began to back up so that I could grab the phone.

"Don't stopppppp, let them call you back," she begged as she panted, out of breath. Deciding that she was right, I ignored my ringing phone and continued to fuck her until we both passed out. When I awoke, Raleigh was still there, snoring softly and entangled in my sheets. With the moonlight shining through the windows, she looked like an angel. Looks were deceiving. Standing to my feet, wearing nothing but a grimace, I walked smoothly over to my patio door and stepped outside onto the deck. The view from the bedroom was one of the things I loved about the house. I could come outside and see the trees, the river, and get a breath of fresh air without even having to leave my bedroom. I was admiring the beauty of nature when I spotted a person's silhouette near the trees.

"The fuck," I said aloud as I walked into my bedroom quickly to grab one of the many guns in my room. I did so much dirt that I had to keep a gun in every room in the house. I would shoot it out with a nigga before I let him catch me slipping.

My loud rustling woke Raleigh. First, she stirred, then she came to a full sitting position.

"What is going on?" she asked as she watched in shock while I loaded the mini-Draco and tossed it over my shoulder.

"Nothing, go back to bed," I grunted while heading back to the patio.

I stepped back outside and swung the rifle from my shoulder.

I aimed and looked into the scope for a clearer view of my target. Whoever was out there was about to meet their maker in a few seconds. I didn't give a fuck who it was. I scanned the area in my scope and saw nothing. Looking in opposite directions to see if I could see someone running away, the only movement I saw was from the trees swaying in the wind. There was no one there. Wiping my eyes to clear them, I continued to scan the area for the shadow. I knew I wasn't imagining shit. However, whoever it was had gotten the hell on and disappeared into the night, so there was nothing I could do about it. Turning back to face her, I placed the large gun on my nightstand and headed into my master bathroom to wash her dried cum from my dick.

"You need to go home before your husband starts looking for you," I told her over my shoulder.

As if I had magic powers, her phone began to ring. I smirked, already knowing who it was. Taking a deep breath, she scooted to the edge of the bed and began to get dressed. When I came from the shower with the towel wrapped around my waist, she was sitting on the edge of the bed, fully dressed, still on her cell phone.

"Yeah, me and the girls had a few too many drinks at the spot on Third Avenue, and I lost track of time, babe. I know I promised to let you FaceTime with the boys before the night was over. My mom is looking after them, and she called me a few minutes ago and said that they were knocked out sleep," she lied to my best friend, causing me to shake my head. Her mom was in Vegas. There was no one looking after her boys but the sandman. She had drugged them with melatonin vitamins so they could sleep while she went out to get her pussy pounded.

"Your sons are fine, Qyleek. You haven't been gone from them but a day," she smiled like a doting mother and wife, even though she was terrible at both jobs. I'd just slept with her a few hours before, and her six-year-old boys were home alone. Bitches really weren't shit.

"I'm only twenty minutes away. As soon as I get there, I'll call you. Let me get off the phone; I'm passing a cop car. It's against the law to have the phone in your hand while you're driving. Wouldn't want to end up like Shovi's girlfriend, sitting behind bars," she smirked at me cruelly.

"Love you too." She ended the call and tossed it into the chair next to my bed.

"Where were we?" She licked her lips, stood up, and walked over to me. "You were heading home. If you leave now, you'll make it in twenty minutes," I dismissed her.

She gave me a look that could melt ice and reached for her purse and keys. "This hot and cold shit you do is getting old, Shovi. Face it, you enjoy giving me the dick as much as I love getting it. Stop fucking me if you're going to bitch up every time your little friend calls my phone. I've never heard of a street nigga with a conscience. If you can't handle what we're doing, stay the fuck away from me," she taunted.

Grabbing her around her throat and slamming her against my bedroom door, I began to squeeze tighter as she looked at me fearfully. "I ain't your husband. Don't come at me with the drama. She clawed at her neck, trying to dig her nails into my skin so I could release my grip. She would break one of those thin ass nails before she caused me to let go.

I smiled as I continued to squeeze the life from Raleigh. When her eyes began to roll back, I moved my hand from her throat, and she fell to her knees. She began to cough uncontrollably as she tried to catch her breath.

"Be thankful I'm a street nigga with a conscience. You were a few seconds away from never laying eyes on your twins again. Now get the fuck out of my house," I smiled at her cruelly. Too afraid to say anything back, she hurried to her feet and half ran down the stairs and out of the door. Putting my Draco in the closet, I walked over to the pants I wore earlier and searched through my pockets. When I finally located my phone, I went back to my missed calls to see whose call I had ignored for a piece of pussy. The caller ID read Qyleek. Rubbing my hands down my head, I realized that Raleigh was right. If I was going to start acting guilty every time I fucked her, I needed to just stay away from her. I would return Qyleek's call in the morning and just lie and say that I was sleeping. Wired from the action, sleep was the furthest thing from my mind. It was still a little early, so I decided to slip into a pair of jeans, a T-shirt, and a pair of Prada sneakers to head to Joe's. I called Bak to see how his trip was going, only to learn that he and Cami had returned to Philly this morning. I invited my day one nigga out to have a drink with me. What I'd been doing with Qy's wife, getting rid of Zay, and the situation with Glow were all eating me up inside. I felt like a bottle of champagne that had been shaken while the cork was still inside. I needed to release and pour my heart out to the only person I knew wouldn't judge me. I had already told Bakari that I had a thing for a woman I couldn't have, but we never got into specifics. Things were getting beyond my control, and I needed his opinion.

After finally making it inside and finding a few seats at the bar, I ordered a Bourbon neat and waited for my best friend to walk through the door. Thirty minutes later, Bakari rubbed his hands together for warmth as he rushed to get inside from the cold air.

"Bak," I called out, causing him to look in my direction and smile while heading my way.

"What's up, twin?" he questioned as he held his hand out and pulled me into a one-armed embrace.

"Shit, I can't call it," I replied while signaling for the bartender to come over so I could order him a Hennessy straight.

He sat down excitedly, and he began to smile for no reason. He looked like a nigga who had gotten his first piece of pussy, and his skin even had a slight glow. His vacation with his bitch must have gone amazing, and I found myself briefly longing for what he and Cami had. The moment was brief. There was no way I could be satisfied with one bitch, when God had given me hundreds of options. It would be ungrateful of me to tie myself to one when God himself wanted me to be fruitful and multiply with multiple women.

I had explained this concept to Bakari a million times, and he clearly didn't agree with me. I decided to tease him for his happiness because I was jealous on the low.

"Damn nigga, I can see all thirty-two of your teeth, and you glowing like a pregnant bitch in her first trimester. Cami turned you into a soft, in love ass nigga," I laughed.

"Fuck you, nigga. Just worry about making me look good when you do the toast at my wedding. I proposed to Cami, and the best man always has to make a speech during the toast." He caught me off guard, almost knocking the wind out of me.

"You proposed marriage? Like some forever type shit?" I asked him while looking at him like he had three heads. "It might be a little too soon for that. Slow down. You have plenty of time for that stuff. She must have been pressuring you by bringing up marriage twenty-four seven. I hate when women do that shit. They start getting older, their clocks start ticking, and they lose their minds," I told him angrily as I picked up my glass and took another sip. Now that he was engaged to be married, he might look at me sideways for banging another nigga's wife.

"She didn't pressure me into nothing. In fact, in all the time we've been together, she's never brought up the subject of marriage. We don't have all the time in the world, nigga. We ain't getting no younger. You want to still be out here chasing hoes when you're old and grey? You're going to end up somebody's fly ass sugar daddy," he laughed.

"When you get a bitch that's rocking with you, all these hoes don't excite you no more," he tried to school me.

"Hennessy straight," I told the waitress as he continued his romantic, Dear John speech.

"I remember when Qy told us he was ready to wife Raleigh. I was sitting where you are, looking like you're looking. Why settle down with one bitch when you can have as many as you want at your disposal? That's what I asked him, and it took me until now to understand his answer. Sometimes a bunch of women just don't do it for you no more. When you find somebody you know is strictly yours, it's a different type of flex."

"I've been fucking Raleigh," I cut him off before taking a huge gulp of my drink. He was driving me insane with this love narrative, and I needed to bring him down a notch or two. He was about to make the same mistake Qyleek did, and in a few years, a nigga would be banging Cami while he was at home playing house. He sat in his seat, staring at me with his mouth open, like I had just told him I was Michael Jackson reincarnated.

"I'm happy for you. You can marry whoever you want. As for me, none of these bitches are getting my last name. The main ones you think are all yours, turn around and fuck your best friend," I shrugged nonchalantly.

He looked like he wanted to speak, but he didn't have the words, so I continued, "Zay found out that we were messing around when he came over to my house unannounced. He tried to blackmail me into leaving Glow alone. Find another trafficker in exchange for him keeping the secret between us," I told him angrily.

"Don't tell me." Bakari found his voice before I cut him off again.

"Yep, I wasn't taking that chance. First, it was too close to the shipment date. I'd been wasting my time and energy, making Glow fall for me, and I didn't have another person to drive in case that plan fell through. Besides, his goody two shoes ass didn't have a sheisty bone in his body. As close as he and Qyleek were, there was no way he would keep something like that to himself. You saw the way he was acting the day Qy told us that he felt like Raleigh was cheating. He stayed behind after the meeting to be the shoulder for a grown ass man to cry on," I told Bakari.

"How did you do it? Did he suffer?" he asked me sadly.

"I didn't do it personally. I sent my young niggas at him to handle it. They shot up the car and it flipped off the road," I replied.

After a few seconds of silence, Bakari spoke again.

"Cami's pregnant. I'm about to be a father. I don't want to raise my seed in a broken home like mine was. I grew up with nothing. I didn't come from a rich family like you did, and I'm stopping that cycle with me. I have more than enough money to take care of my family and make sure they don't want or need for shit."

"Well, just be with her! You don't have to put the court in your business and marry her ass," I reasoned with him.

"Just being with her ain't enough. I hear what you're saying, but she's not Raleigh, and I'm damn sure not Qyleek. I trust Cami. She tells me everything, even the embarrassing shit about her. Like the fact that Glow's first love is Princeton's father. Her mother doesn't even know that shit, but she confided in me. She's different. If I find out she's fucking another nigga, I'm going to kill her and the nigga too." He shot me a look of warning. "But I highly doubt it will come to that; she ain't on no sneaky shit like that," he finished. I held my hands up in mock surrender. "She ain't my type," I smirked at him playfully.

He laughed at me and shook his head. "So, what the hell are we going to do about this? I talked to Qyleek earlier, and he told me that someone in Dubai told him that he spotted a guy who looked just like Zay at this hotel in New York. When he leaves from Dubai in the morning, he's going to head straight to this hotel to see if anyone at that hotel has seen him. I don't think he's ever going to give up looking for Zay. Do you know where the body is? If we can find the body, we can move it somewhere in the open and spin the narrative. If we can give Qyleek some closure, he'll stop his search and let it go, just like the police have. Xavier had enough money to disappear, leave everything behind, and start over. Since they haven't found a body, they don't have any evidence of foul play. They're on to the next situation. You would think Qyleek would have given up by now," Bakari told me. Just like that, he'd gone back to being my best friend and not judging me for the fucked up moves I made. I'd just told him that I had one of our best friends and business partners killed, and I was fucking the wife of our other best friend. And he was sitting here, helping me figure out a way to sweep all of my dirt under the rug.

"Zay's body can't be too far from Dead Man's Curve by his house — that's if the animals haven't gotten to his ass by now," I retorted.

"Ok, first thing's first. We deal with this Zay situation to get Qy off the trail. Afterwards, you have to set Raleigh up with another nigga and let Qy catch them. You and I both know that when that nigga gets a hunch, he's like a dog with a bone. He's going to follow that shit through. I'd rather he catch his bitch with another nigga than let him catch her with you. If he plays himself off the street behind his hoe ass wife, that'll be his loss. Instead of splitting our business three ways, we'll only have to split it two," he smiled at me while raising his glass.

"My nigga," I smiled, while clanking my glass to his.

Chapter Five

Cami

A day after returning home, I was in the middle of lunch with Raleigh when I received a call from a private number. "How the hell does this nigga keep getting my number?" I asked aloud, already knowing who it was before I answered the call. I stood from the table at The Cheesecake Factory in Center City. Raleigh and I had just left Chuck E Cheese's, and after playing games for hours, the boys were enjoying dessert. We engaged in small talk while we enjoyed midday cocktails.

"Can you keep an eye on Princeton for me while I take this?" I asked Raleigh nicely.

"Sure sis, go ahead; I got him," she waved me away dismissively.

I jumped from the table and ran to the ladies' room while answering the phone in aggravation.

"What the fuck do you want? Why are you calling my phone? You did your damage and ended a twenty plus year friendship. Now can you go back to wherever the hell you came from?" I demanded.

"I'm not going anywhere. I want to meet my son and have a relationship with him. My plan was always to return to Philly if professional baseball didn't work out. Now that I have my doctorate in Psychology and steady clients, I'm ready to build my private practice and close with a realtor on my first home. I can't wait for you and Prince to see it. The house I'm closing on makes the one you're living in with your little boyfriend look like a shack. I'm here to stay, and I'm ready to be the father to Princeton that I know I can be," he persisted.

"Princeton doesn't *need* a father," I told him, putting an emphasis on the word need. "He has a father already— my fiancé and the father of the child I'm carrying is Princeton's father. He even calls Bakari daddy; he doesn't know you exist, and I don't want him to know about you. Move on with your life. Princeton is living proof that your nuts work; go find another bitch and get her pregnant. Get married, run off into the sunset, hell, join the circus. I don't give a fuck what you do; just LEAVE US ALONE!" I yelled loudly.

Sean was my weakness and with him around, I knew it would only be a matter of time before I ended up in a compromising position. I had everything I needed in Bak; he was a provider, a protector, a confidant, and as close to perfect as a bitch could get. The dick was insane, the head was murder, and he was fine as hell. I had finally checked off every box on my list when it came to a soul mate, and he was it for me. However, lust was a powerful thing. The same lust that had allowed me to fall into the trap with Sean initially even though he was off limits, would be the same lust that caused me to fuck up a good thing with Bakari.

"I can't do that, Cam. You kick this fake hate shit for me, but I was the one who paid your tuition through community college. Or have you forgotten? You had no problem calling me private to ask for money before you got with this nigga you're with. Now that you have a golden ticket to take care of your ass, it's to hell with the trade school I paid for, and fuck the times I've sent you money for Princeton?!" he yelled back angrily.

"You sent the tuition check the day I posted on social media that I had enrolled in school. You didn't put a return address because you knew I would send it back if I knew where to send it to," I argued.

"You could've torn it up; you didn't have to use it," he

retorted.

"You gave me money twice for Princeton. Two times, I called and asked you for money, and that was when I was in college, and I wasn't working. He's six years old, and I haven't asked you to do shit since he was a few months old. I've been handling my business as a mother long before I got with Bakari. You keep saying you've been a check, like I've been taking money from you consistently," I argued back as tears rolled down my cheeks. My betrayal had landed me stuck with the baby daddy from hell, and I had no one to blame but myself. All I wanted was to peacefully move on from my mistake with the man of my dreams, but my past was biting me in the ass and wouldn't let up.

"I could've consistently sent you money for him, but you blocked me, so that was your fault. Speaking of shit that's your fault, I hate to have to do this to you, but you pretty much haven't left me with a choice," Sean told me before I heard moaning sounds that sounded a lot like me.

"What the hell is that?" I asked him angrily.

"*I want me, you, and Princeton to be a family,*" I heard his voice.

"*Princeton and I have a family with Bakari, and you and me were sneaky links that resulted in a slip up. I don't know how many times I have to tell you that to get you to understand,*" I heard my voice as I put my hand over my face in annoyance. This nigga had recorded us the last time he was at my house, which was the night of my ladies' get together.

"This is insurance," he replied as the video continued to play in the background.

"Hold up. This is my favorite part right here," he told me excitedly as I heard the sound of my bed squeak and remembered the moment all too well. That was the moment when I had weakly pushed him off me and allowed him to push me on the bed.

"I watch this every night," he told me seductively as tears filled my eyes.

"I cut the video at the part where I'm sucking your pussy with your legs wrapped around my head," he laughed menacingly. "Every time I see you in this little cute pajama set, my dick gets hard. I remember back in the day we couldn't keep our hands off each other. Don't no nigga know your body like I do." His words cut me like a knife.

"Now, I'm sure your hubby wouldn't like this video if I showed it to him. His future wifey getting her pussy eaten by her baby daddy is enough to make any nigga snap," he threatened.

"What do you want?" I whispered weakly. "What would it take for you to make the video disappear and for you to get out of my life?" I questioned.

"Where are you?" he asked.

"The Cheesecake Factory in City Center," I replied as I wiped the tears from my face.

"See you in twenty minutes. I'll call you when I'm outside," he replied before hanging up in my face. I went over to the sink and splashed cold water on my face to hide the fact that I had been crying. Placing my Louis Vuitton oversized bag on the counter, I pulled my Fenty liquid and powder foundation from my purse, as well as my Mac eyeliner so that I could retouch my makeup. I couldn't let Raleigh see that I had been crying because she would want to know what was wrong. With her husband being one of my fiancé's best friends, I had to be careful of what I told her. I didn't know if she was the type of bitch that pillow talked with her nigga and told him everything. If she were Glow, I could pour my heart out and never worry about a word I said coming back to bite me in my ass.

My mind then drifted to Glow. When Bak told me not to ask questions I didn't really want the answer to, I didn't bring the situation up to him ever again. How he'd known that I was at the furniture store, worked out in my favor. I wasn't sitting in a jail cell with Glow rotting away, and that was thanks to him. She was some type of friend to go out of her way to invite me on a run while she was trafficking drugs. I had a son, and I was pregnant. I couldn't be a mother from behind a glass wall. It was fucked up that she would even put me in that situation.

Dismissing Giovanni from my thoughts, I took my time and applied my makeup. I couldn't let Sean's sadistic ass see me sweat. He was getting a kick out of torturing me, but he had the right bitch. I would play along with his little game while I thought of the perfect plan to get him the fuck out of my life for good. I wasn't that same old college girl that he'd dicked down years ago. I was a grown ass woman now. If he wanted to play dirty, I could do that.

When I finished up in the ladies' room, I washed the makeup from my hands and headed back to the table.

From afar, I could see Raleigh smiling widely as she held the phone to her ear. She looked like an excited schoolgirl as she tugged at the edges of the thin Chanel scarf around her throat. Personally, I hadn't seen a woman tie a scarf around her throat since the eighties, but it paired nicely with her vintage Chanel dress. The only thing that could make a woman smile like that was a man she was crazy about. Her body language showed that whoever she was talking to had her head all the way fucked up. Walking back to the table quickly, I took a seat in my chair, and she jumped out of her skin. When she looked at me, she looked like she had been caught with her hand in the cookie jar.

"Sorry it took so long," I laughed it off.

"Tell my brother Qyleek I said what's up. He got you damn near about to jump out of your skin. Let me speak to him. I want to know how his trip to Dubai was. I might drag Bakari's ass out there for my birthday. Maybe Qy could recommend the hotel he stayed in," I rambled as I reached for her phone to talk to Qyleek.

She backed away from me like I had shit on my hands, and I was about to smear it on her Chanel dress.

"Um, he can't talk right now; he's busy," she replied hurriedly.

"Love you, babe. See you at home later." She hit a button to end the call and put the phone in her purse quickly. "Hello? Raleigh?" I heard a man's voice say. She had pressed the button so quickly, she'd accidentally put him on speaker phone instead of ending the call. She pulled the phone from her purse, and I saw Shovi's name across her phone screen. She ended the phone call and threw the phone in her purse angrily. Looking at her strangely, I shook my head and laughed it off. There was something going on there, but I had enough shit going on in my life to worry about other people's issues.

Suddenly, my phone rang, and the caller ID read *Private* across my phone screen.

"Could you hold Prince down for me a few minutes? I have to meet a friend to grab something, and I don't want to take him away from his dessert. His ass hasn't looked up since the waiter sat the cake down in front of him," I joked.

"Sure, no problem," she replied sweetly.

"Thanks sis," I replied fakely before getting up from my seat and heading out the door. When I stepped outside, I heard a horn honk, coming from a green Range Rover. Rolling my eyes, I walked over to the truck and pulled the passenger handle, getting inside. I was glad the truck had tinted windows so no one could see who was inside.

"*Sean, stopppppppppp,*" I heard my voice call out over the recording. Sean had his long, thick dick in his hands, and he stroked it slowly as he watched the video of us. I looked at him in disgust. As handsome as he was, I didn't understand how he could be such a creep. I was sure he had bitches beating down his door to fuck with him, and he was looking over all of them. Instead, he wanted to torment a woman who was happily taken. It really was true that men obsessed the most over what they couldn't have.

"Could you turn that shit off and put your dick up? You're acting like a weirdo, and I hate that for you," I shamed him, causing him to look at me sideways.

"My shit hard as a rock; I can't just *put it up*," he mimicked.

"Come here and do that thing I like, and it'll go down," he smirked.

"Cut the bullshit. What do you want from me to make this shit go away?" I turned in the passenger seat and looked at him angrily.

He reached over and slid his free hand up my thin dress as he began to stroke his dick slowly. I swatted his hand away, and he gave me a look of warning before reaching over and doing the same thing again. Sliding my panties to the side, my pussy was already moist from watching him play with his big, beautiful dick. It looked like a king-sized Snickers with the veins popping from it.

"I told you what I want you to do," he replied.

"But—"

"No buts. Give me what I want, and I will go away."

"I can't do this shit with you, Sean." I begged my son's father as he fingered me slowly, causing my back to arch and my toes to curl. My dumb ass had given him the worst thing you could give a nigga like Sean — ammunition. I gripped the side of the passenger seat as he pleasured both me and him at the same, steady pace.

"You're already doing it, Cam," he moaned.

"Fine, when do you want to do this? The sooner we can get it over with, the better," I retorted as the rest of the attitude I had slid away. It was replaced by lust.

"Now," he smirked.

I scowled at him as I removed my panties from underneath my dress.

I then crawled to the back seat and spread my legs as wide as they could go. He came behind me and lifted one of my legs over his shoulder before sliding his dick inside of me slowly.

He gritted his teeth as he bit down on his lips. Pregnant

pussy was a nigga's weakness and judging by how he was reacting, I could tell that this was his first time fucking a pregnant woman. I was the mother of his child, and we'd never fucked when I was pregnant. I was too busy hiding from him, for him to get to experience this feeling. I saw the whites of his eyeballs as his thrusts became quicker. I couldn't deny that I was enjoying the sex as much as he was. Sean was my first everything. He knew my body like the back of his hand. He was hitting my G-spot, and I tried my hardest to hold the moans inside, but every time he went deeper, my back arched, and I moaned his name.

"That's right, bitch, don't hold it in. Let me hear that shit," he replied roughly as he continued to fuck me slowly.

That was all the push I needed. Sean knew that I loved to be degraded while I was getting fucked. It was a kink that I had never shared with Bakari because I didn't want him to look at me weirdly. Sean had discovered it on accident, and after realizing it made me wetter, he made sure to incorporate it into his sex talk.

"I'm cummiinnnnn', Sean," I moaned. My head was saying no, but my body was saying yes. A few seconds later, I screamed out as my orgasm overtook me, and I dug my nails deep into his flesh. Sex had become a million times more intense since getting pregnant. My hormones were all over the place, and I was always horny.

He put his hand over my mouth to muffle my screams, and that turned me on more. I popped my pussy on him and locked my legs behind him to keep him in place. He began to jerk violently, and I knew he was cummin'. His soft thrusts turned harder as he plowed into me deeply. When he was finished, he collapsed, lifeless and sweaty on top of me. Suddenly, my senses returned, and I felt sick to my stomach. I couldn't believe I had just fucked another nigga while I was pregnant with Bakari's baby. The whole thing had happened so fast, but I instantly felt ashamed.

"Get off me!" I yelled out and pushed Sean with all my strength. He smiled at me weakly as he took deep breaths to slow his breathing.

"Just like I remembered," he joked while reaching for a pack of baby wipes, grabbing a few out, and throwing the pack at me. I grabbed the wipes and began to wipe his cum off me and freshen myself up. What grown man, who wasn't the father of a toddler, had a large pack of baby wipes in his car? A grown man who knew he was going to get some ass. He had already planned this shit out.

"Are we good now? Are you going to leave me and my family the fuck alone and go back to where you came from?" I questioned.

"Nah, I told you earlier I'm sticking around here," he smiled at me slyly.

"But I know what I do want from you next, though. I want to meet my son. Unblock my number so I can text you with the day and time."

"I don't mind sharing you for now, but sooner or later, you're going to have to put on your big girl panties and break it off with Bakari. I ain't too crazy about taking care of another nigga's baby, so you can wait until after you have the baby and just leave it with him. Then, you and Princeton are coming home. Now get the hell out of my truck and expect my text message. It'll be sometime this week," he dismissed me.

Angrily, I put my panties on and grabbed the door handle to get out of his truck.

He pulled out of the parking lot, and I smoothed my hair down before walking back into the restaurant.

When I walked up to the table, Raleigh smirked at me. "Your hair is fucked up. What did you have to get from your friend?" she asked.

I didn't reply, and she laughed.

"I'll keep your secret if you keep mine," she smiled.

"I don't know what you're talking about." I played dumb while reaching for my mirror to see if my hair was out of place. It wasn't. I looked over at her, and she laughed. She was testing me to see if I would give myself away.

"Made you look," she laughed while clutching her stomach.

I reached into my purse and threw down a few bills on the table to pay for lunch. "Come on, Princeton, your play date is over," I told my son as I pulled the napkin from out of his shirt that kept the cake from spilling all over his Gucci outfit.

"Let's do this again soon," I smiled fakely at Raleigh while grabbing my son's hand and leaving the restaurant.

That bitch was messy, and when the slick shit she was doing with her husband's friend hit the fan, I didn't want to be anywhere near the commotion it would cause. I needed to keep my distance from her ass. I was back at square one with no one to confide in, friendless, and missing Giovanni. I cried silently all the way home. When I pulled into the parking lot, I didn't see Bakari's car. Figuring he must've gone out with Shovi, I thanked God that I had beat him home. I then hurried inside to our master bathroom to take the hottest bath I could handle. Sean hadn't even used a condom. I needed to make an appointment with my OB-GYN next week to get tested for STDS and check on my baby. I had to get Princeton's father the fuck out of our lives because as long as he had ammunition against me, this wouldn't be the last time he'd force me to do whatever he wanted. After cooking dinner, I went into my room and went to sleep. I felt an intense sadness coming, on and sleep was the only way I could escape from the messed-up situation I was in.

Chapter Six

Glow

The next morning, I was on demon time after realizing that Shovi had played me. I was about to spend a good amount of my life in prison behind some shit I truly had nothing to do with. I would lose the career I'd worked so hard to get as well as my amazing apartment. My mother wouldn't be able to afford my car payments and hers, so my Lexus would be going back to the dealership. All of the things in my life that I had taken for granted because I was so hung up on finding someone to love, would be taken from me because of one stupid ass mistake. I wanted a bitch to try me because I had a lot of anger I wanted to release. I didn't give a fuck if I lost my life in a jail brawl; I was hurt at how easy I had been manipulated for love. As if the devil knew I was ready for some action, the first person I laid eyes on when we were released from our cages was Frita.

I had found the perfect hiding spot for my makeshift weapon — in the waistband of my pants near my lower back. I could feel the pointy edge sticking me in the crack of my ass with each step I took. She was laughing and joking, surrounded by her flunkies, the same bitches who had jumped me, but I was so blinded by anger, I didn't give a fuck.

When I made it closer to her, I placed my hands behind me, prepared to slice the black off the burly bitch when suddenly, she smiled at me. Her smile wasn't an intimidating grin like the one she'd given me before. This time, it was genuine. It could have even been described as friendly. Confusion swept through me as I looked at her in the eyes, trying to figure out what her angle was. "My bad about that shit yesterday; it was all a misunderstanding," she told me while shrugging her shoulders.

"I don't understand," I replied because I couldn't understand how overnight, this bitch had gone from hating me and knocking my face into the concrete to smiling at me and apologizing to me in front of everyone. Jail was weird, and these women had to be mentally ill.

"You don't have to worry about nobody fucking with you, Glow. You good in here." She dismissed me and walked away with the group of bitches walking behind her like a bunch of puppies. I stood there, in shock for a few seconds then headed to chow. I still didn't let my guard down, though; I had made that mistake once, and I wouldn't make it again.

Later that night, I lay awake, listening for anything that sounded out of place. I held my weapon tightly in my hand and took slow, deep breaths. When I heard footsteps stop in front of my cell door, I moved from my back and sat upright on the cot. The door made a low noise as it creaked, and I slid to the edge of the bed to prepare to do what needed to be done. I was sticking bitches first and asking questions later. To my surprise, CO Brooks stuck her head in the door and slipped into the room.

"This is for you," she told me hurriedly while putting something in my palm and walking away. She slammed the heavy door behind her.

When I looked down, it was a Samsung flip phone. Throwing it on the cot like it was poisoned, I jumped up and stared at it like it was about to grow legs.

These bitches are trying to set me up, I thought to myself. It was illegal to have a cell phone in jail. That was considered contraband, and I could get into serious trouble. I didn't understand why they had it out for me so bad, but I was about to make some noise and wake the entire block up — until the phone began to vibrate quietly.

Walking over to it, I flipped it open and began to read the text message that had come through.

Whatever you're thinking, forget about it. I'm here to help you because you don't deserve what happened to you. I heard you had a little trouble in there, but that's over with. As long as you're there, you don't have any worries. Good night.

Looking at the screen like this was all some sort of prank, I read the message over and over again. I decided to call the number to see who the hell it was. When I dialed the number, the phone rang for so long, I eventually hung up. Trying the number back, the same thing happened again. Going over to the contact list, I was surprised to see that my mother's number was saved in the phone.

I texted her and told her that I loved her.

"I love you too, my beautiful girl," she replied, causing tears to fill my eyes. This really was legit. My mother was the only person who called me that. If it were a set up, they wouldn't have had her number pre-programmed into the phone.

Placing the phone under my pillow, I silently thanked God, the universe, The Three Stooges, and whatever guardian angel I had sitting high and looking down on me.

Every night at that same time, the same number texted me and asked if I was good. Every night, I had a full conversation about my day with a complete stranger. I'd tried to call the number over and over, but it just rang incessantly. No one ever answered, and it never went to voicemail.

"Loosen up your grip a little bit. Damn Frita, you're about to snatch my brain out," I complained as I sat between the legs of my once enemy and got my hair braided two weeks later.

"My bad, Glow. I'm heavy handed as hell, and you know that already," she joked as she loosened her grip on my scalp. I was getting a fresh set of braids for my first court appearance after being locked up for three weeks. I was nervous and excited at the same time, while praying for the best possible outcome.

"Yeah, I know personally how heavy handed your ass is. It took forever for those bruises to fade off my face. Too bad this ugly ass scar is permanent," I shook my head sadly. I went out of my way to avoid mirrors just because I knew that it would be there, staring back at me. A constant reminder of the accident I had in the U-Haul that had mutilated my face. A constant reminder that I had been a fool for a nigga.

"The scar doesn't take away from your beauty; it only shows people that you been through some shit. Wear your wounds with pride. Also, I'm sorry about that again. I was on some dumb shit, but me and the girls are praying that court goes well for you today," she apologized sincerely.

I turned my body back slightly to look at her face and thanked God that I didn't have to use the weapon I created for her.

Frita had been true to her word. Not only had I not received problems from her, or anybody else, during my jail time, but bitches were going out of their way to be nice to me. They had gone from treating me like shit on the bottom of a shoe to treating me like I was Griselda Blanco, the Godmother herself. It became even weirder when I began to receive special attention from the correctional officers. They were kissing my ass just as hard. Correctional Officer Brooks, who had once screamed at me like I was trash, now made random conversation with me like we were old friends. My books were so full of cash, I couldn't even spend it all. It was like I'd died and gone to the twilight zone.

"It's cool. I'm not one to hold grudges," I told Frita. "What baffles me is that at first, you were ready to rip my head off for no reason. Now, you're sitting here, braiding my hair, and you've been incredibly kind to me. People don't usually have such a big change of heart so quickly. Be real with me, what ended your issue with me?" I questioned.

She looked slightly uncomfortable before saying, "You have some powerful people looking out for you." She then turned my head back around so that I could prepare for my court date.

Thirty minutes later, CO Lee came to my cell and banged her stick on the bars. "You're up, Henderson," she told me before putting her key in the gate to unlock it.

I first had to go to the visitation room so that I could speak with my mother and lawyer before my arraignment trial. They were pushing to get me bail since this was my first offense, and it was non-violent. I wasn't a flight risk since I had a job and ties to the community. I sat in the room with my ankles chained to my wrists like Hannibal Lecter as I waited for them to come into the room. When my mother walked in, tears instantly began to form. She'd been rocking with me for these past few weeks. Every night and first thing in the morning, we prayed together on the phone. Throughout the day, she sent me uplifting text messages to keep me encouraged, and she was a constant source of strength. I tried to stand to hug her, but the male guard CO Lee had passed me off to, gave me a look of warning. Not willing to let him spoil my joy, I smiled and waved at my mother from my seat.

"Hey, mom," I greeted her.

"Hey, my beautiful girl," she greeted me. I had been hearing those words every night, and it felt good to finally hear them in person. I knew that I was anything but beautiful with this ridiculous scar on my face. However, she was my mother, so I was sure that I was still beautiful in her eyes. After she stepped fully into the room, I looked behind her, expecting Mr. Dowler, the bald, short, white guy who wore bifocals and jacked up pants. My mouth dropped in surprise when Lisa Gibbs walked through the door.

I recognized her from her billboards. Lisa Gibbs was that bitch in the city. A thick BBW, she had enough ass and hips to spare. I would have killed to have her body. She wore a tight dress and six-inch heels, serving classy and professional, while still being sexy. She was the most well-known and expensive lawyer in Philly because she had never lost a case. A lot of people claimed she slept with judges and court personnel, but nobody had any proof. The rumors didn't stop her bag; they only gave her more publicity while she laughed all the way to the bank. Whatever her methods were, her clients' cases were always dismissed, and she was always booked. I had no idea how the hell my mother had pulled this off in the time frame she did, but I didn't have any complaints.

"Hi, Ms. Gibbs, it's a pleasure to meet you. I love your commercials on TV," I complimented her as I reached out my hand to shake hers. She shook my hand while smiling at me. "It's a pleasure to meet you too, Giovanni. Your mother has told me so much about you. I have all of the information I need on your case, and I can assure you that I will get you bail at your hearing today," she told me before sitting down in her seat.

After discussing our plan of action, what she wanted me to say, and sharing a few laughs, the meeting was over. My mother handed me the clothes she'd stopped by my apartment to get for me. I walked into the courtroom, feeling one thousand times more confident about the outcome of my case.

With my head held high, I maintained my composure while the district attorney painted me out to be a heartless, drug trafficking, threat to society who needed to stay locked up to keep the streets safe. It took everything in me not to spazz. The shit he'd said was completely disrespectful. The only crime I had been guilty of was falling for someone who had ulterior motives. Looking at the judge's face, I knew I was doomed. He had eaten the shit the district attorney had fed him, and he was now looking at me in pure disgust. Hanging my head, I prepared for him to deny my bond and send me back to my cell. When it was attorney Gibb's turn to speak for me, I prayed that she was worth what she was charging as I watched her intensely.

Fifteen minutes later, tears poured freely down my face as my spirits were lifted. Lisa was worth double of what she'd charged. She spoke so highly of me that I began to see my own worth again. She had even called in multiple witnesses to attest to my character. My next-door neighbor, the owner of the private practice I worked at, and my landlord all stepped up to talk about what an amazing, driven, and kind young woman I was. At this point, I couldn't stop the tears if I tried. I had never known that the people I saw every day thought so highly of me. When she was done with her argument, the judge had set my bail at forty thousand dollars and banged his gavel. I was going home. I knew the battle wasn't over, but I cried tears of joy as I laid my head on the desk and released the burden that had been on my shoulders. Attorney Gibbs had carried the torch and placed it in my hands. Now, it was up to me to take it all the way. There wasn't a chance in hell that I was about to go down for Ta'Shovi's shit. My freedom was my opportunity to take his snake ass down. He had played with the wrong bitch.

Later that night, I sat in my jacuzzi Whirlpool tub and let the jet streams massage the kinks from my back. I hadn't had a hot bath in weeks, and it felt so good to sit down and wash my body without having a bunch of women around. I sipped a glass of expensive wine as I relaxed in the comfort of my own home. When someone rang my doorbell, I almost jumped out of my skin. I hadn't let anyone know I was out, and I told my mother to not let anyone know as well. I wanted to fly under the radar for as long as could while I decided the best course of action to clear my name. Quietly, I stepped from the tub and tiptoed through the house. When I made it to my door, I looked through the peephole, but I didn't see anyone there.

"Bad ass kids, playing at the door," I said a loud to myself, dismissing the doorbell ring as a prank. Before I stepped from the door, something on the porch caught my eye. It was a small cardboard box. Opening the door, I quickly grabbed the box and shut the door behind me. I walked the box straight to my kitchen table and sat it down. I had watched enough horror movies to know that fingers, a small foot, or any other miniature body part could be in this little box. I shook it a few times to see what would happen. When nothing happened, I began to slowly open the flaps. I was filled with surprise when I opened it, and there was a small notebook that looked like a planner.

"Who in the hell would send me a planner then run from the door?" I asked myself in annoyance as I flipped through the book to see what was inside. As I read through the planner, I noticed familiar names, places, and dates. Someone incredibly close to the nigga that played me, had just given me exactly what I needed to clear my name. I smiled. Who said God didn't answer prayers?

Chapter Seven

Cami

"Not tonight, babe," I told Bakari as I pushed him away and denied him sex for the third time this week.

"What's up with you, Cam?" he asked me in annoyance. He was wearing nothing but a towel wrapped around his waist. Bakari looked good enough to eat. I had to give credit where it was due. My fiancé had the sexiest body I had ever seen on a man. His chocolate skin was covered in tattoos, dreads pinned into a sexy man bun, and his deep, brown eyes made my stomach ball in knots when I looked into them. We'd been fucking like rabbits since the night we met. He knew I couldn't keep my hands off him. If I continued on this path of turning him down for sex, he would start to get suspicious. I couldn't even blame it on my period; I was four months pregnant and hadn't seen Aunt Flo in quite some time.

"Nothing, I'm just not in the mood. I'm pregnant and hormonal, can't you understand that?" I flipped it on him as I turned over in the bed. The truth was, Sean had begun to frequently blackmail me for pussy since the day I saw him at The Cheesecake Factory last week. I had gone and dug myself in a deeper hole, because he recorded us fucking in his car that day. Now he had multiple recordings of sex with me, and he was threatening to expose me to Bak if I didn't give him what he wanted. I'd heard the saying that men knew their pussy and could tell if their woman had been sleeping with someone else. I didn't know if it was true, but I didn't want to take the chance. I'd been turning Bakari down to keep him from finding out that I was consistently sleeping with someone else. I was stuck sleeping with my stalker, obsessed baby daddy and withholding sex from the man I loved. Sean hadn't even asked to meet Princeton again. He'd gotten so strung out on the pussy, he'd forgotten that a relationship with his son was his original reason for blackmailing me.

I wanted nothing more than to tell Bakari what was going on, but I knew that he would go upside my head if I told him that I had been seeing another man. I could've confessed to him when Sean broke into the window and forced himself on me initially, but I was in too deep at this point.

"I'm sorry, baby. I guess I am being selfish," Bakari told me sadly as he sat on the edge of the bed. "You're carrying my seed, and I don't want to make you uncomfortable. Is there anything you and the baby are craving right now?" he asked me sweetly while reaching underneath the blanket to grab one of my feet. He placed my foot in his lap and began to massage it softly, being sure to pay careful attention to the spot that gave me the most issues. I was incredibly flat footed, so my feet always hurt where my arch curved. He knew this without me saying a word. This was what I was afraid of — two years of being in a relationship with him, and this man knew my body too well.

"Actually, I have been fiending for some Kosher dill pickle chips and some heath ice cream with the candy chunks, caramel, and chocolate swirls," I lied to him.

"No pressure, I'll run to the store and grab that for you," he smiled at me and stood to his feet. He walked into the closet, grabbed a pair of grey sweats, and paired it with a T-shirt and a pair of slide-in Yeezy's. His dick print poked out through his sweatpants, and my pussy began to throb. The only time I'd gone a week without Bakari inside of me, was when it was that time of the month. His dick wasn't as huge as Sean's. The thickness and length were comfortable and the perfect size, which made sex with him so enjoyable.

"Stop looking at that; you don't want it, remember?" he joked when he caught me staring at his print. "I wasn't looking," I lied terribly, causing him to laugh, jump on the bed, and begin to tickle me. I laughed and fought him off playfully. After rolling around, I ended up wrapped in his strong arms and staring at him face to face. He stared at me intensely, like he was trying to commit every detail of my face to memory. He then took his index finger and began to trail from my temple, down my nose, and to my cheeks, before tracing the outline of my lips.

Tears filled my eyes. This was the perfect moment to tell him what had been going on. Maybe if I was just honest with him, he wouldn't hate me, and he would help me with the Sean issue. All I had to do was find the courage and just tell him.

"Bakari" I started as my hands shook nervously, and I stared at him, eye to eye.

"Yes, beautiful?" he replied while still tracing my face with his fingertip.

"I… I ummmm…" I struggled to get the words out. They were caught in my throat, and I couldn't get them to make it past my lips.

"I love you," I told him while reaching out to rub the side of his face.

"I love you," I repeated.

I wanted to make sure that he understood that I loved him with all of my heart, because when this shit came out, I would lose him, and he would never look at me with this much love in his eyes as he was doing in this moment.

"I love you more, Cam. You mean everything to me. I'm so glad that you're the mother of my child, and you agreed to be my wife. You have a nigga being all mushy while I'm trying to maintain my image out here," he laughed, causing me to laugh as well as the tears flowed from my eyes and down my face.

"Even the hardest nigga still has a heart, and you have mine. Don't ever break it, mama." He looked at me intensely while grabbing my hand from the side of his face and kissing my fingertips.

"I'm about to go and grab this nasty ass shit you want to eat, but what did I tell you about crying? If my baby is born with crooked eyes because you keep crying, you might as well prepare to sit down nine more months. I'm giving you another one before this one can talk, if you can't understand the assignment the first time around." He kissed me and wiped my tears from my face before getting off the bed.

"Ok, no more tears. Just hurry back with the ice cream," I demanded.

Grabbing his car keys from the nightstand, he walked out of our bedroom door, and a few seconds later, he walked out of the front door, and the alarm beeped.

When he was gone, I placed the pillow over my face to muffle my screams as I cried into the pillow. I prayed to God to keep my baby safe. With all of this pressure I was under to please a nigga I hated, while not getting caught by the man I loved, there was no wonder I hadn't had a miscarriage.

The next morning, I received a text message from Sean, whose number I had saved in my phone under Stacey.

Today is the day. I'm ready to meet my son

The message caused me to roll my eyes in annoyance. Unfortunately for him, Bakari had paid for tickets for him, Princeton, and I to go to Disney on Ice. The tickets were nonrefundable and incredibly expensive. Bak didn't half step, and when he took us to the show last year, we had floor seats. He would've paid to have us on the stage with the characters if he could. No expense was too high for him when it came to putting a smile on Princeton's face.

I can't today

I texted him back quickly as I looked over my shoulder to make sure Bakari wasn't near. I was in the kitchen, making breakfast for Bak and Prince, and when we finished breakfast, Bakari was taking us shopping to buy us both something fly to wear. Afterwards, we would grab some lunch and catch the show around three p.m.

What the fuck do you mean you can't?

Sean texted back in less than a few seconds.

I didn't text back, and my phone began to ring, startling me. Forwarding the call, I continued to turn the bacon in the skillet to make sure it was crispy enough on both sides. My phone began to ring again, and I quickly answered it while walking out of the door and closing the door behind me.

"I can't talk right now," I answered angrily. Bakari could walk up at any moment.

"I want to meet my son today at four p.m.," he replied coldly.

"We have plans with Bakari. He bought tickets to a show months ago, and the show is today. Are you really going to continue to use this over my head forever? I'm sick of this shit," I told him angrily.

"If you're talking about the tickets to Disney on Ice, I bought tickets as well when I found out they would be in town. I wanted to surprise you. I bought a ticket for you, Prince, and me to go enjoy the show like a family," he laughed with delusional, sending chills up my spine.

"I told you—" I began before Bakari pulled the door open quickly and stuck his head out the door.

"I'm hungry, woman," he told me.

My heart began to pound, and I felt lightheaded as I waved him away dismissively.

"I'm on the phone; I'll be inside in a minute," I told him,

hoping that he would catch the hint and walk away. He stood on the outside of door and folded his arms.

"Yes girl, that's your husband's crazy ass friend, interrupting my conversation. Are you bringing the twins to the Disney on Ice show, Raleigh?" I laughed while pretending to talk to Raleigh and thinking quick on my feet.

"That nigga must be standing right there," Sean questioned.

"Yeah, Bakari took us last year, and we had the best seats. Princeton really enjoys it; the twins will too," I answered his question while keeping the conversation going.

"Does that nigga know I make you scream my name when I'm inside of you? I bet he doesn't make your pussy squirt like I do. I know he don't knock your walls down. I stretched you all the way out. My dick is bigger than his, I can tell. Tell me he doesn't fuck you like I do," Sean taunted while Bakari stared at me intensely. I felt like I was about to faint as my hands shook nervously.

"Better yet, give him the phone; let me tell him," Sean laughed menacingly in my ear.

"You are a trip, Raleigh. Let me warn you now, girl. The food and drinks are high as hell in the arena, so you might want to feed the twins before you get there. Bitch, I'm talking four whole dollars for a bottle of water," I laughed fakely as I stared Bakari in the eyes.

"Fine. Forget about the show. I'll sell the stupid ass tickets. I want you in my bed tonight, ten o'clock sharp, bitch. We have some things to discuss. Don't be late, or your hubby gets all your home videos." He hung up in my ear.

"Well, let me go, girl; I gotta feed my man and my son. Bakari is standing here, staring me down like he wants to rip the phone from my hand. I'll hit you up when we get to the arena, so we can speak before we go to our seats," I told myself because there wasn't anyone on the phone. Pretending to hit the button and quickly putting the phone in my pocket, I walked past Bakari and back inside of the house.

"Are you ready for me to fix your plate, babe?" I asked Bak sweetly.

"Hell yes. I'm about to starve. You outside on the phone, chit chatting with your friend, while your husband is hungry," he complained.

"My husband is not handicapped; he knows how to pick up a plate and put food on it. It's already cooked; the hardest part is out of the way," I replied.

"I don't make the plate like you, and you know it. You know exactly how much to give me, how much seasoning to add, and all the rest of the spices to make the plate hit. When I fix my plate, I always get too much food or oversalt it," he smiled at me.

"I'm going to have to call Qyleek and tell him he ain't keeping his wife busy enough, because she's cutting into my family time. Y'all are always together, and I'm starting to get a little jealous of all this hanging out y'all have been doing. When I introduced you to her, I didn't know she was going to turn my wife into a city girl and always have you outside," he joked while pulling me closer.

"First off, your wife been a city girl; that's what you love about me. Don't act like you not a city boy because you and Sho-V are always outside. When I want to get cute with my friend and go out, you want to complain," I laughed loudly.

Since I didn't have anyone else to hang with, I needed an excuse when I was at Sean's beck and call. I'd been using Raleigh as my alibi. I knew I said that I was done with her, but since I knew her secret, I figured I could use it to my advantage. That bitch had better clear my story because I would gladly spill the tea if she didn't have my back if the topic ever came up.

Later that night, as Sean huffed and puffed on top of me, I prayed for him to nut quickly so that I could get back to the house. Thirty minutes earlier, I had cooked pork chops smothered in gravy, mashed potatoes, sweet corn, and dinner rolls for dinner.

Me and my cute little family sat around the dinner table and shared our favorite parts of the Disney show as I sipped a glass of wine. While Bak was drowning the pork chop in hot sauce, I was waiting patiently for the two crushed Tylenol PM's I'd slipped into his plate to take effect. I'd also crushed a melatonin vitamin and slipped it in Princeton's food. I needed them both to be snoring and slobbering on their pillows when I slipped out of the door to go to Sean's house.

When they were finally asleep, I used the address he gave me and pulled up to a beautiful mansion a few minutes outside of Philly. He was right; he could sit my house inside of his. If I had ever doubted that Sean was paid, I now had all the proof I needed. After all, he was a doctor; I just didn't understand how he could be a therapist and be as crazy as he was. Maybe all of those years of talking to crazy motherfuckers had rubbed off on him. His weird ass was not normal.

"I'M CUMMMMINNNNN'" he moaned loudly in my ear, as I did a Kegel on the dick. I clenched my pussy muscles tightly to send him over the edge. As soon as he fell on top of me, I pushed him off and quickly began to put on my clothes. I never stuck around for a second longer than I had to when we were finished.

"Before you rush off, like you hate to be in my presence any longer than you have to, I told you that I needed to discuss something with you. I now know what I want you to give me to get rid of the tapes," he told me as I sat on the edge of the bed, getting dressed.

"I'm listening," I answered in annoyance.

"I will give you the recordings I have and delete all the copies if you give me fifty thousand dollars," he told me simply, as if he'd asked me for fifty dollars.

"Are you crazy? I don't have that type of fucking money," I retorted.

"I know you don't. You're just a housewife, but your hubby

does. I've done my research on Bakari, and he's not the small-time punk I thought he was. Weed Hut is a million-dollar franchise with multiple locations throughout Philly, and I read somewhere that the owners are about to open a location in Cali as well as in Atlanta. The biggest names in the entertainment industry are promoting Weed Hut and saying that they stop in a store to shop whenever they're in Philly. Meek Mill just posted a picture in front of the store to his millions of social media followers last week! The stores are doing very well, and Bakari's money is longer than I thought. I realized today that I'm tired of sharing you with him. I thought I could wait until you had the baby, but I'm tired of sitting on the sidelines while another man gets to enjoy my family. Glow is in jail, we're both older and wiser, and we have a son together. Nothing is stopping us from being together. This game is getting old to me. I've had all the fun I want to have," he told me while rubbing my back.

I moved away from him and stood to my feet. "What does you wanting me have to do with me stealing money from him?" I questioned.

"I need to focus and get my private practice started. I don't want to touch my savings or get a loan from the bank, so why not make your hubby pay me for fucking and sticking a baby in what belongs to me? If he's who you want, pay me to keep this quiet, and he'll never have to know you were unfaithful. You can just tell him you fell out of love with him," he shrugged.

"That's fucked up, Sean." I rushed out of the door quickly and headed to my car. Sean was loaded, and he didn't really need the money; he was just trying to get me to steal from Bakari. Despite what he believed, Bakari was a street nigga who wouldn't take too kindly to being stolen from. If I robbed him for fifty grand, I wouldn't have the option of telling him I "fell out of love" with him. He would either put a bullet in my head or never trust me again. Both outcomes were terrible, and they worked out perfectly for Sean. He had figured out that I wasn't strong enough to leave Bakari, so he'd come up with a way to make him leave me.

Chapter Eight

Bakari

I'd watched Cami crush pills and put them in both me and her son's food at dinner last night. The minute she stepped away from the kitchen, I switched my pork chop in the simmering pan and pretended that I'd gotten up from the table because she hadn't put enough Tabasco sauce on my meat. If I wasn't worried about harming my child, I would've put the piece of meat on her plate and put her ass to bed.

I pretended to stretch and yawn and headed to the bed, so I could see what she was about to do. She came into the room a few minutes later and stood silently by the door to see if I was really sleeping. I snored loudly until I heard her leave the house, and her car pulled out of the driveway. I waited a few extra minutes then got out of bed. I went to grab a drink and fired up a blunt to calm my anger. There had to be a reason why my bitch was sneaking out of the house and putting sleeping pills in my food. The million-dollar question was, *where in the hell was she going?* I peeped in Princeton's room to check on him. He had one foot where his head was supposed to go and the other, hanging off the bed wildly. I smiled at him. I really loved the little dude and went out of my way to show him how much I cared. I did the same for Cami; that was why her actions were baffling to me.

"What is your mother up to, Prince?" I asked aloud. He farted in response, causing me to laugh out loud. Closing his door behind me, I went to have a seat in the dining room as I contemplated how best to handle this situation. Part of me felt like I deserved what she was doing. After all, I'd let Glow suck my dick not too long ago, and I never told her what happened.

That shit wasn't my fault. She came on to me, and it never happened again, I thought to myself.

The question was, how should I handle this situation, knowing that I hadn't been completely truthful with Cami either? Should I sit here and wait for her sneaky ass to walk in the door like a parent catching their teenager after curfew? She could easily lie to me, and I would never know where she'd been or what she'd been doing. Should I question her about it tomorrow to see if she would tell me the truth? After a few more drinks, an entire blunt, and a lot of pondering, I decided that the best way to fool a fool, was to act like a fool. I would let her think that I had no idea what she was doing and give her enough rope to hang herself.

The one thing she wasn't lacking was audacity. I couldn't believe I went for her telling me she "wasn't in the mood" for sex. She just hadn't been in the mood for sex *with me.* I began to question all of the shit that was right under my nose. Maybe that was the nigga I caught her on the phone with earlier. My heart told me it wasn't Raleigh because Cami was shaking like a leaf. Since when did she need to go outside on the porch to take a phone call?

"All these bitches are the same; ain't none of them getting my last name," Ta'Shovi's voice played in my head.

"Cami isn't like that. She tells me everything," I told him. Now I was questioning that statement. Did I really know the woman I was about to marry?

I looked at my phone and the clock read 11:30 p.m. She'd been gone for an hour and a half. I sprayed air freshener to cover up the smell of weed and went into the bedroom to lay down. Twenty minutes later, I heard the alarm beep, signaling that someone was coming in the house. I felt like a woman staring out of the window, waiting for my cheating spouse to come home. Ta'Shovi was right, my love for her was turning me soft.

When she snuck into the room, she went straight to the

master bathroom and got in the shower. That was cheating signal number one. Aside from the sneaking around, what had she been doing that required her to immediately get into the shower when she made it in the house?

When she crawled into bed next to me, she stayed on the opposite side of the bed with her back turned to me. If she had turned around, she would have seen my eyes wide open, staring at her. Instead, she kept her back to me and cried softly for hours before falling asleep. When I heard her soft snores, I pulled her close to me and kissed the nape of her neck.

"Don't worry, babe. I'll put you out of whatever misery you're in," I whispered in her ear, before closing my eyes and going to sleep.

The next morning, Cami snored softly in my arms. She had a late night, so I knew she would sleep in. Getting out of the bed, I went to check on Prince, who was sitting in the living room, watching cartoons on the flat screen.

"Morning, dad," he greeted me.

"Morning, son. Are you hungry?" I asked.

"Yes, can you make me cereal?" he grinned at me mischievously. Cami made breakfast for him every morning because her mother had done the same for her growing up. As a kid, he preferred cereal. I would always sneak at least one box of cereal in the house for him.

"Of course," I smiled back and poured him a bowl.

While he ate, I freshened up. After slipping into a pair of jeans, a T-shirt, and sneakers, I returned to the living room, where Prince was still transfixed by the cartoons.

"Turn off the TV and go pick out something to wear; we're going to have a boys' day," I told him.

Without a second thought, he turned off the TV and headed

to his room. He was an amazing kid, and he always did what I asked of him.

After getting him ready, I grabbed Cami's keys so that I could take her car instead of mine, and we headed out. I stopped at Best Buy to grab a tracker to place on her car. I then took it to get washed, detailed, and filled it with gas. While we were heading to the house, sipping on milkshakes, Ta'Shovi called me.

"What time are we linking up to handle that?" he questioned.

"I'll meet you at Joe's in thirty minutes," I replied before hanging up.

I hoped when we made it home, Cami would still be asleep so I could change the settings in her phone. I had bought some technology that would allow me to get every text message she received; and every time she got a call, I would receive a notification. Before I flew off the handle, I wanted to have solid proof that she was fucking around. As I told Ta'Shovi the other day, she wasn't Raleigh, and I damn sure wasn't Qyleek. I wasn't about to sit around and cry about what a grown woman was doing with her pussy. I loved her more than my next breath, but if I found out she was out here moving foul, I would end her ass without hesitation.

Thankfully, she was still sleeping when we returned. I went into her purse, grabbed her phone, and installed the software. I then went into the room and shook her shoulders gently.

"Wake up, sleepy," I coaxed her.

"Hey babe, what time is it? How long have you been up? Do you want me to make you some breakfast?" she asked.

"I'm good, babe. Me and Prince went to get some food. I let you sleep in because you seemed hella tired," I taunted her.

"Yeah, this baby is throwing my sleep schedule all off. I was up half the night, watching TV while you were knocked out. When I finally did get to sleep, it was really late," she lied to me easily.

I wondered what else she had lied to me about this easily.

"All these bitches are the same; ain't none of them getting my last name," played in my head.

"Yeah ok," I replied before moving away from her before I did something I would regret.

"Princeton is wide awake and full of sugar, so you might want to get up so you can find something for him to do. Maybe another play date with Raleigh and the twins," I told her.

"I have to go check on the stores; I'll be home later." I walked away without a hug, a kiss, or even saying goodbye. I was supposed to be keeping up pretenses so I could catch her in the act, but I couldn't help it. I wanted to be away from her quickly before I caught a domestic violence charge.

"This was the spot where they ran the nigga off the road," Ta'Shovi told me a few hours later, as we rode slowly around Dead Man's Curve. My body sat in the passenger seat of his Tesla, but my mind was a million miles away. Every time my phone beeped, I reached for it quickly to see if it was a notification from Cami's phone.

"What's up with you, nigga? Your head is all the over place," Sho-V told me while looking at me sideways.

"Just been thinking. When's the last time you talked to Raleigh?" I asked him.

"I was with the bitch yesterday. I had to choke her ass a few days ago. She thought she was going to talk to me like she talks to Qyleek, but I had to let her know I'm not her husband. She got her attitude together and came crawling back a few hours later," Sho-V laughed before taking a sip of his Simply Fruit Punch juice that he spiked with tequila.

"Yeah, gotta put these hoes in their place," I agreed.

"She was supposed to meet Cami at the Disney show yesterday, but Cami said she never showed," I fished for information.

"She hired a babysitter to take care of the kids for the day yesterday. The girl took them to the show and kept them for the day while their mother sucked and fucked me. It ain't no way one nigga can handle her sex drive. I had to fight her ass out of my house first thing this morning. My dick was dry, sore, and tired from all that fucking. A nigga is in his thirties now. Like I told her, I'm not one of these high school boys with nothing to do besides fuck. I don't have the energy I used to have," he told me in annoyance.

"So, you and Raleigh were together the whole day yesterday, and she even spent the night at your place? She never left your sight? Where the hell was Qyleek?" I questioned him in surprise. They were taking serious chances and being too sloppy. If they were going to have an affair, it was supposed to be a wham, bam, in and out type of thing. They were asking to be caught.

"Yes, we were, and no she didn't. She told Qy that she had a chef's writing convention she had to go to in D.C. She left her car with the babysitter and rented a car and everything. These women are smart as hell. Qy was so busy following up on a tip he received from the worker at the Hotel in New York, he didn't even question it," Sho-V told me as he pulled over to the side of the road. We'd dressed comfortably, so we could do a walk to see if we could see anything over the cliff.

"Oh, ok. Well, just be careful. I think you should keep her as close as possible for the next few days while we set her ass up," I told him. I wanted to see how far Cami would take this "I was with Raleigh" lie. I now knew that wherever she was last night, she was there alone, because her alibi was at my best friend's house, getting fucked while her husband lay in bed, alone, just like I did.

When we finally found a trail that was safe enough to hike down, we walked around in the woods until we were tired, sweaty, and sore. Just before we gave up, I spotted something far off in the distance.

"What is that?" I asked as I squinted my eyes and wiped the sweat from my brow.

"It looks like a car!" Sho-V exclaimed while running in its direction.

I followed behind him. When we made it to the car, it was indeed Zay's truck. The truck was fucked up, mangled, and half burned like the engine had caught fire. Bending down to look inside, I tried to see if I could see a body inside, but the air bags had deployed, and the top was crushed. If Zay was still inside of that truck when it landed, he was dead, and his body was stuck inside of the rubbish.

"We can't get inside of that fucked up car and get his body out of there," Sho-V said.

"Yeah, there's no way he made it out of this shit," I replied.

"We'll come back later and set this bitch on fire a little more then pay a homeless person to say they found the truck; it'll just look like he wasn't paying attention and ran off the road. Hopefully, that'll be enough for Qyleek to leave this shit alone," Sho-V told me.

After leaving a burner phone near the car so we could know exactly which spot to come back to, we made the long trek back to Sho-V's car. We jumped into the car and sped off quickly, not knowing that we were being watched.

Chapter Nine

<u>Cami</u>

When I finally awoke from my coma-like sleep, I took a hot shower and got dressed. In his own world, Princeton sat on the couch, playing his Nintendo DS that Bakari had bought him.

"Hey, big head. Are you hungry?" I asked him as I walked up to him and rubbed my hands through his thick, wavy hair.

"No, I'm still full from Bakari making me breakfast. Mom, we had a boys' day; you missed all the fun!" he told me excitedly. His eyes lit up bright like Christmas as he told me about how he rode around and ran errands with his dad, and it made my heart happy. He was proof that it didn't take the most expensive thing for a father to impress a child. He was happy, simply riding around with Bakari and being treated like a big boy.

"Did you hear me, mom? Then, we went to the electronics store and daddy bought some stuff. Then, we went to get your car washed," he told me.

"Well, since you had so much fun with daddy, I guess you don't want to go run errands with mama then," I told him, faking sadness.

"I didn't say that," he told me while smiling and showing the gap where his front tooth should be. I smiled and grabbed my purse, as he raced out of the door. When my phone rang, I assumed it was Bakari without looking at it and answered while locking the door. "I'm up, babe," I laughed while hitting the key fob to unlock the car door.

"That's good to know because I know I wore your ass out last night," Sean replied, causing me to snatch the phone from my face and look at it in disgust.

"I thoguht you were someone else. What is it, Sean?" I asked angrily. My entire mood had gone from happy to miserable in the span of a second.

"Damn. Well, good afternoon to you too. You were just excited a second ago when you thought I was your weak ass boyfriend; now you want to sound all depressed and shit," Sean acknowledged.

Not bothering to respond to his analogy, I held the phone so he could tell me what he wanted from me.

"Ok, no response. I understand. Well, I called to tell you that I'm going to be needing that money sooner than later. I'm standing outside of one of your hubby's stores right now, and I see him standing behind the counter. Maybe I should walk up to him and show him this video."

"Please don't!" I screamed out, startling Princeton, who was grabbing at the car door handle at that same moment.

He dropped his hands like I had just told him a bomb was inside of the car, and he turned around to look at me.

"No, not you baby. Get in the car," I told him, causing him to give me a crazy look. He looked even more like his father when he made certain facial expressions, and the fact that Sean had re-entered my life, forced me to see that Princeton was his exact replica.

"Oh, that's my little man? Tell him daddy said what's up. As a matter of fact, I want to meet him today. As soon as you go to the bank and get out the fifty grand I asked you for," he persisted.

"There is no way I can just walk into a bank and take out that much money from my fiancé's account at one time. I thought that you would give me time to gradually give you the money in increments," I complained.

"Do I look like a layaway plan to you, bitch? You are not about to make payment plans with me. Get the money NOW!" He hung up in my face.

Shaking my head, I walked over to the car and headed towards the bank. I was an authorized user on all of Bakari's accounts, so I could try to take the money from various accounts and go to various banks. I knew they would alert him to what I was doing, but I didn't have much of a choice.

"Change of plans," I told Prince as I got into the car. "We're going to make a few bank runs and pay some bills. How does that sound?" I asked my son, faking excitement so he wouldn't get alarmed.

"Bills are boring. See, this is why I like hanging out with daddy," he replied while sitting back and pulling his Nintendo out of his backpack.

"You better be lucky I ain't taking your ass to the middle of the street and running you over with my car, out here looking like the demon that's ruining my life," I mumbled under my breath.

After multiple bank runs and riding to a bunch of different ATM locations, the most I'd made it to ten thousand dollars. Next up on my list was stepping into Winsler Financial. Bakari had a few hundred thousand dollars in his account with them, and I figured it wouldn't be hard to get around five thousand dollars from that account.

"Come on, let's go inside," I told Prince, distracting him from his Game Boy.

"Maaaaa, another bank? We still ain't paid all the bills?" he complained. He was ready to do something fun, and I couldn't blame him. What almost seven-year-old would be ok with riding in a car for hours, going from ATM to bank? Turning to face him, I tried to reason with him. "We've paid all the bills; I just don't have any extra money to take you to Pizza World. I guess we can just go home, and I can whip up some chicken soup," I shrugged my shoulders while turning around and cranking the car up.

"PIZZA WORLD?! Why didn't you say that to begin with? Come on, mom, let's go inside and get some money." He eagerly took off his seat belt and laid his game on the seat next to him. I laughed and got out of the car. I walked into the bank, holding his hand.

"It's an amazing day at Winsler! How can I be of service?" the bank teller greeted me. I had to give credit; the customer service was on point. All of the staff wore big, smiling faces like they genuinely loved their jobs. The atmosphere was professional, there was a server in the lobby, going up to customers to see if they wanted something to drink while they waited, and I noticed from the large picture of the owner, this establishment was black owned. Feeling proud of my people, I turned my attention back to the teller.

"Sure, I'm an authorized user on my fiancé's account, and I would like to withdraw money," I told her.

"No problem," she smiled at me while typing into her computer.

"Hey, little man," she greeted Princeton, and he waved back shyly. I smiled at him.

"Go ahead and place your debit card into the machine and enter your pin number," she instructed me. I followed her orders and typed my pin number in. Suddenly, her face went from smiling and happy go lucky to screwed.

"This account has been temporarily frozen," she told me with a slight grimace.

"That can't be possible," I replied.

"Do we still get to go to Pizza World?" Prince asked while tugging on me.

"Hush, dammit!" I snapped on him, causing everyone to look at me like a piece of shit mother. I was mortified.

"That can't be possible. Can you please check again?" I fixed my tone and begged the teller.

"There's nothing I can do to this account without the owner present. I can give your husband, the owner of this account, Mr. Bakari, a call and have him come down here to unfreeze it. He's been banking with us for years, so we would hate to cause him any dissatisfaction. Give me a quick second to go to the main office and reach out to him," she told me while moving away from her computer.

"No, that won't be necessary," I told her before snatching my card from the bank machine and grabbing Princeton by the hand. I stormed out of the bank and walked quickly to my car.

When I laid eyes on my car, I screamed loudly.

The word *SLUT* had been spray painted in red all over my white Audi Q3 SUV.

"What the fuck?" I looked around to see if I saw anyone, but there was no one there. Too embarrassed to go back in the bank, I put Prince into the car, got inside, and sped off towards the house. I picked up my cell and called Sean.

"Hi there," he answered the phone with glee.

"I couldn't get all the money. I was only able to pull out ten thousand until he froze one of his accounts. I'm guessing he knows, but he hasn't reached out to me. Can I just bring this to you, and you give me a little time to get the rest?" I begged.

"Quick second, Mr. Bakari. This is the wife," Sean told somebody in the background, causing chills to go down my spine.

Chapter Ten

Glow

Account balance : $10,600.00.

I opened my Wells Fargo app the next morning, and I almost passed out. I hadn't been to work, so I wasn't expecting a paycheck. I had foolishly spent all of my savings to get sexy for a nigga who hadn't really wanted me in the first place. I'd missed my surgery because I'd been in jail for almost a month, and all of the money I'd invested was nonrefundable. I had six hundred dollars to my name before I went to jail. I expected less than half of that amount to currently be in my account. I'd given my mother all of my passwords and pin numbers so she wouldn't have to use her own money to keep money on my books. It was bad enough she'd used all of her own savings to get me the cheap lawyer I had before. I had no idea who was footing the bill for Lisa Expensive Ass Gibbs, because I knew her work wasn't pro bono. Now there was this. Ten thousand dollars had been deposited into my account the day I was released.

I covered my mouth as tears of joy filled my eyes.

"Thank you, Jesus. I don't know who's making this happen or how, but thank you, Lord," I cried as I logged into the rent cafe and paid my rent for two months. I then went over to PECO and paid my power bill down to a zero balance. I did the same with my cell phone bill, gas bill, car insurance, and credit card bill. This was usually my routine when I woke up on pay day, but this money hadn't been deposited into my account from payroll.

I was left with eighty six hundred dollars after I paid off all the past due balances and every other bill in my house.

Getting out of bed, I headed down to Hertz rental to rent a car. I didn't want to move my car from my mother's garage. I also hadn't powered my cell phone on. I was still working off the burner phone that the corrections officer had snuck to me that night. For the first night in weeks, the unknown number hadn't reached out to me to see how my day had been. My heart told me that it wasn't a coincidence that the first night I didn't get a text message was my first night out of jail. I had no idea who was looking out for me, but I hoped that it wasn't Ta'Shovi going out of his way to help me because of the guilt he felt for getting me in that fucked up situation. He was going down regardless.

While I was standing in the line at Hertz, I noticed a familiar person a few people ahead of me.

"Hi, Ms. Raleigh Hudson, how are you?" The agent greeted Qyleek's wife, whom I had met at Cami's slumber party. I wondered how things had been going with Cami's "new bestie".

"Not you knowing me by name like I'm a regular here," Raleigh laughed loudly. I recognized that laugh immediately. It was weird and high pitched, exactly like the one I'd heard in the background when I called Ta'Shovi. Turning my face to the side, I listened deeper.

"We have to take care of our repeat customers," the agent kissed up to her.

"I wish Suki Yun down at the nail shop felt like that, babe. I've been going to the same nail tech for three years, and she charges me for every single thing and acts like she doesn't know who I am every time I sit in her chair," Raleigh complained.

I rolled my eyes at her selfishness. There was a reason I didn't like this bitch when I first met her at Cami's house. She was an attention seeking whore, who did too much and acted like she was cuter than she actually was. Plus, the way she said *babe* sounded exactly like the bitch I heard in Sho-V's background the last time I called him. I then remembered Qyleek mentioning that she was cheating on him, and it all made sense. I prayed, for his sake, that he figured everything out sooner than later. Cami had been parading my first love's child around me, directly under my nose for six years. Sometimes, the people you assumed were friends were nothing but enemies in disguise.

"Mhmmm." A woman standing behind Qyleek's wife cleared her throat to remind the bitch that her little friendly chat was holding up the line. Sucking her teeth in annoyance, she ended her conversation and handled her business. When the agent gave her the keys to the rental, she tossed her long hair over her shoulder and walked out of the Hertz building like she owned it. She put an extra sway in her hips as she walked so her ass could jiggle.

"Extra for no reason," I said to myself as I moved up in the line. When I was done getting a car, I put the address into the GPS and headed to where all the bullshit had taken place. I recognized the first address in the book immediately upon opening it, so that was where I'd start. The shady ass furniture store in Rhode Island had been a front the entire time. The manager had pretended to be nice, pulled out the red carpet, and treated me like royalty while he filled the Uhaul truck with drugs. His crooked ass was going down right along with his business partner, Ta'Shovi. Entering the store, I noticed a few people shopping for furniture. I passed the same bed that Cami had sank into.

"This bed is so damn comfortable; you're going to have to carry me out of here on it, or I'm not leaving." I heard her voice in my head as I rolled my eyes and looked around the store. I saw the same sales associate from last time, but I didn't see the owner, Abdul. I walked up to the sales rep.

"Hey, is Abdul around? I need to speak with him about something." I asked the same Arab sales rep who helped Cami and I the first time we came. He was smiling at me like I was a customer who was in need of help and acting professional like this shit wasn't a huge drug front. Or maybe only a few of the employees knew what was going on right under their noses, and he foolishly believed he was only selling furniture.

This nigga don't even remember me, I thought to myself.

"Sure, have a seat in his office, and I'll tell him you need to speak with him," the sales rep replied.

Walking over to where Abdul had come from the first time we met, I went inside the office and shut the door behind me. It was sparsely decorated with a large office desk, a chair behind it, and a chair on the opposite side of the desk. There was a file cabinet up against the wall, with one of the drawers hanging open. Instead of going to sit in the chair, I walked over to the file cabinet and pulled out my phone. I began to snap pictures of documents that looked important. After going through the entire file cabinet, I walked over to Abdul's desk and looked through the paperwork. I took pictures of everything I saw on the desk while shuffling through the papers. When I noticed what looked like a secret door on the opposite side of the office, I walked over to it and tried to open it. In the midst of prying at the door, I didn't know I wasn't alone until I felt something pull over my head.

I screamed loudly and fought the air, but it was no use. I felt a needle being stuck into my arm as I heard someone talking in a different language.

What the fuck have I gotten myself into? I thought to myself and, everything went dark.

Chapter Eleven

Cami

"Sean, please don't tell me you're talking to Bak," I told him as I switched lanes and tears filled my eyes.

"Honey, I haven't made it to Whole Foods yet; I stopped in this cool store because I wanted to see what they have. We both have passed this store a million times, but I have never been inside to see what they actually have," he taunted me.

"Sean, I have ten thousand dollars right now. I can meet you at the park, give you what I have, and introduce you to your son if you please just walk away from him. I'm sure we can come up with a solution," I swallowed hard. My head was pounding because I hadn't eaten or drank anything in all day, I felt nauseous, and my emotions were all over the place.

"Meet me at Callaway Park in fifteen minutes," he told me.

"Hey, thank you for all your help. I will be seeing you again," Sean told whoever he was talking to, causing me to take a deep breath. "See you in a few," he hung up in my face.

Slowing down my speed before I plowed into someone, I rerouted so that I could make it to the park.

"I'm sorry about yelling at you back there, baby. Mommy is just under a lot of stress. I love you so much," I told a silent Princeton, who hadn't said a word to me since we left the bank.

"It's ok, mama. You haven't had anything to eat. You'll feel better after we get pizza," he forgave me and turned on his Game

Boy.

"We have to make one quick stop first. Mommy's friend wants to meet you for a few seconds. Promise to be nice and don't mention this to your daddy, ok?" I asked him.

"Ok," he told me sadly.

When we made it to the park, there were kids running around playing, parents on the side watching them, and a few people jogging.

I noticed Sean sitting on one of the benches with a blanket over his lap and a book in his hand. I rolled my eyes and grabbed Prince's hand to head over that way.

When I apporached, he smiled at me. I reached into my purse and handed him the envelope of money angrily.

"Thanks, lovely lady," he smiled at me.

"Who do we have here?" he asked, looking down at Prince.

"My name is Princeton," Prince introduced himself respectfully.

"Hey Prince, would it be ok if I call you that for short? My name is Sean." He stuck out his hand to shake Prince's, and he put his little hand into his and shook Sean's hand while never breaking eye contact.

"Wow, who taught you how to shake hands like that?" Sean asked him while smiling.

"My daddy taught me," Prince told him nonchalantly.

"Mom, can I go play? I see one of my friends from school on the swing," he turned to me.

"Sure, but be careful. We won't be here long," I told him as he ran off to say hello to his friend.

Sean looked at me angrily like he wanted to chew my head off.

"So, he's calling that bitch ass nigga daddy?" he questioned.

I took a deep breath in annoyance but didn't answer.

"Have a seat next to me." Sean flipped the blanket back and patted the seat.

"No thanks, I'd rather stand," I replied.

"It wasn't a question," he replied angrily.

Sitting down next to him, he flipped the cover over both of our laps.

"Unbutton your pants," he commanded.

"Sean, my son is a few feet away," I spat.

"I know that; that's why we need to make this quick," he told me.

Unbuttoning my pants and unzipping them, Sean reached over into my lap. He then stuck his hands in my pants and began to rub my pussy through my panties.

"Look at me, MA!" Princeton screamed out as he swung on the swing next to his friends.

"I-I see you, baby," I stuttered as tears filled my eyes.

Sean slid my panties to the side with one finger and used the same finger to separate my lips. When he made it to the opening, he stuck his finger inside of me and began to rotate it slowly.

"Your shit always so wet," he moaned low enough for only us to hear.

"Get the rest of my money, babe," he told me as he fingered me in a public park with my child less than a few feet away. I had never felt so worthless in my life. When he was finished, he slid his finger from my pussy and brought the finger to his lips. He stuck the finger inside of his mouth and began to suck my juices from it like he was sucking a lollipop. Disgusted, I buttoned my pants, gently moved the blanket to the side, and began to walk away before Sean called out to me.

"Hey, wait!" he yelled, causing me to turn around to see what he wanted.

"Word of advice, if you're having a son, don't make the kid a junior. I didn't know the name Bakari was so common. I actually wasn't talking to your Bakari; I was talking to another guy with the same damn name at a cologne store. Who knew Swahili names had become so popular," Sean said as he went back to reading his book.

Feeling like a fool, I nodded my head and walked over to my son. He looked up at me in innocence, and I looked down at him in shame. I then grabbed his hand and headed back towards the car. People gave me awkward stares as I drove through the city, determined to take my son to Pizza World. Prince was right; I felt a lot better after a few slices of pizza. Afterwards, we headed home. I tried to reach out to Bakari, but he didn't answer his phone for me. I hadn't heard from him all day, so I assumed that maybe he hadn't been alerted to what was going on. No news was good news.

"Don't touch the pan; you have to let the cookies cool off, Prince!" I scolded my son a few hours later. I used the oven glove to take the cookie pan from the oven. I sat the cookies on top of stove so they could cool off and pulled the heat gloves off before reaching for a glass of water that I wished was vodka. I still hadn't heard from Bakari since he dropped Princeton off. He'd never gone an entire day without a text message or call. Maybe that bitch at the bank had still called him when I left and told him that I was trying to take money out of his account. Maybe he was going to walk through the door and put a bullet in my head because I stole from him. Maybe he wasn't going to come home tonight. Different scenarios played in my head, each one worse than the last. I tried to keep a brave face for my little one, but I was dying inside.

"Let me lick the bowl, since I can't have a cookie yet," Prince complained as I handed him the bowl of left over cookie batter. Prince and I were currently baking homemade cookies of different flavors; the house smelled just like a bakery.

Deciding to be the bigger person, I picked up my phone to call and check on Bakari for the second time, hoping that he would answer for me. The same thing happened when I tried to call him earlier — the phone rang until it went to voicemail. I placed it back on the counter and picked it up a few seconds later like a crazy person. I was fiending for some adult conversation. I needed someone to vent to, or at the very least, distract me from the shit I'd been going through with Sean. I didn't have anyone I could talk to who'd understand what I was going through. I was about to pick up my phone to call my mother and check on her when suddenly, my phone began to beep in my hand, signaling that I had a text message.

Opening the message, tears began to fill my eyes when I saw that it had been sent from Sean.

Have the rest of my money in cash in three days, or hubby gets what I told you he's going to get. Oh and go check the doorstep. I saw something on your porch for you.

"I just can't get a fucking break," I said aloud as I dropped the phone like a hot potato.

"Mommy said a bad word," Prince called out to me. I ignored him and ran over to the door and opened it quickly. Laying there on the doorstep, out in the open, were large pictures. The very first one was of me, on my knees, with Sean's dick in my mouth.

I quickly snatched the pictures from the doorstep, shut the door, and locked it behind me.

"Mama, are you ok?" Prince asked me with worry etched across his little face.

"Yeah, mommy's ok. Put on that cartoon movie you like, and I'm going to go and grab something for my stomach," I lied to him as tears rolled down my face.

I bent down, hugged him and kissed him on his cheek.

"Ewww! Mama, don't kiss me; I'm not a baby. I'm too old for kisses," he complained as he wiped the kiss from his face and ran over to the couch while grabbing the remote for the TV. I ran to the back quickly and went into my room, being sure to lock the bedroom door behind me. I then began to go through the pictures. There were over fifty pictures of me in various positions. You could tell the pictures had been taken from a video. As I went through photo after photo, my heart broke into a million pieces. All Bakari had done since he met me, was be a good man and stepfather to my son. He had gone out of his way to make us feel loved and cared for, and I repaid him with the ultimate betrayal. I couldn't bring myself to steal forty more thousand dollars of his hard earned money and put it in another man's hands.

I grabbed the phone angrily and dialed Sean's number. "Why the fuck are you doing this?" I questioned him as the tears ran down my face uncontrollably. I'd tried to stay strong, but I was at my breaking point. I was sick of fighting a battle I was losing, and I didn't see a solution in sight.

"I don't know what you mean," he laughed.

"These pictures, Sean. What if Bakari had come home and seen these pictures? What if my son had run to the car to get something out of there and saw these pictures of me in all these fucked up positions? On my knees, getting fucked from the back, legs in the air, sucking your dick… what if my six-year-old son saw this?" I asked him angrily.

"I have no idea what you're talking about," he laughed.

"You're telling me, somebody has pictures of you in all these compromising positions, and they delivered them to your front door? That's a bold motherfucker right there. You must have a lot of enemies, Cami," he taunted me in a sing song voice.

"I'll get you the money. Will you leave me and my son alone if I do that?" I asked in desperation.

"If you get the money, I won't give your husband the pictures and videos of you being slutted out. I didn't say anything about letting you go. You and me were meant to be together. All of this shit I'm doing is out of love for you," he corrected me.

In that moment, I realized that there was no way out of this. Sean's delusional ass would always hang this shit over my head to use me to do what he wanted me to do. I was too afraid to tell anyone what was going on. I had to suffer in silence until he was through playing this sadistic game of cat and mouse. There was only one thing I could do to gurantee he wouldn't win.

"Fuck you," I told him angrily before ending the call in his face. Standing to my feet, I went into the living room to check on Princeton. He laughed loudly at the Disney Channel movie, and my heart felt full. I was so happy I'd gotten the chance to be this beautiful boy's mother.

I sent my mother a quick text message then went into the garage to grab the rope that Bakari had bought from Home Depot a few months back. I then went to our bathroom and turned on the water for a bath. I would rather die before I hurt the only man who'd ever truly loved me. I'd rather take my life before I faced him. I was so full of shame, and I had no one to confide in who wouldn't judge me for the stupid shit I'd gotten myself into.

Throwing the rope around the bath tub's upper railing, I then placed the other end of it around my neck and tied it as tight as I could. Death would be better than this shit. My mother would take care of my son like her own. I was her only child, and my death would hurt her, but she was the strongest woman I knew. She would hold it together for the sake of her grandson and raise him to be an amazing man. He wouldn't end up anything like his no-good father. My hands shook nervously as I contemplated on really doing this. Could I really take my own life? I'd never been suicidal before. I'd always considered myself mentally stable. I was just tired. I was tired of fighting a losing battle I saw no way out of. Dragging the highest step stool in the house underneath the rope,

I cried for my unborn child, who I'd never meet and who'd never live. Killing myself meant killing my child, but it wasn't like it would matter. When Bakari found out what I'd done, he'd disown the child anyway. I was actually doing the kid a favor. Wrapping the noose around my neck, I tied the knot as tight as I could and kicked the step stool from underneath me.

Expecting it to happen like the movies, I thought my neck would snap instantly from the weight of my body. I was surprised as I felt the irresistible urge to cough. I began to choke as I clawed at my neck, and the rope restricted my air flow.

WHAT THE FUCK ARE YOU DOING?! YOU WANT TO LIVE! my mind yelled at me. It was the same mind that had just convinced me that I had nothing left to live a few minutes before. The will to live suddenly appeared inside of me. Ten thousand dollars, blackmail, cheating, or love weren't worth my life. I would always have the love of my children, and they were all I needed. I began to kick and thrash wildly while trying to call out to Princeton for help. He couldn't hear me; he had the cartoon movie turned up loudly, and I was in my bedroom with the door shut, inside of my bathroom with the other door shut. I had also turned on the bath water to keep him outside of the door. I had executed this plan a little too perfectly as I tried my hardest to snatch the rope from the wooden upper railing, but it was secured too tight. I fought as hard as I could until I had no more fight in me. My eyes began to grow heavy, and I felt like I was drowning. There was nothing else I could do but to give in to the darkness that had been trying desperately to pull me under.

Chapter Twelve

Bakari

I had finally finished helping Ta'Shovi handle torching Zay's truck. Instead of going to find a junkie to call in the tip, we concluded that it would be best to not have any loose ends. Instead, I called in an anonymous tip from a burner phone, pretending to be a camper. After I told the police I'd found a burned car, and gave them the address, we went through the nearest camp site and jumped into a rental car that Ta'Shovi had convinced Raleigh to rent for us. When we left the scene, I went back to Sho-V's place to shower and freshen up. Slipping into a pair of changing clothes, I went into his TV room and sat down on the large recliner chair. I then pulled out my phone and turned the power on. I didn't want the cell towers to pick up that I'd been anywhere near the area where Zay's car would be found.

The minute I turned the power on, I received notifications back to back.

A withdrawal of 2,500 dollars was successfully taken from your account.

A withdrawal of 500 dollars was successfully taken from your account.

A withdrawal of 1,500 dollars was successfully taken from your account.

I received so many noticifaction on my phone, I began to feel like I'd been the victim of identity theft. I went over to each banking app and checked the accounts the money was missing from. True enough, the money had been deducted from the balances. Suddenly, a light bulb went off in my head, and I went over to the app I was using to track Cami's whereabouts. I noticed that she'd been at different ATM locations and banks all day.

Maybe she found the tracking device on her car, and she's trying to get enough money to leave me since she knows she's caught, I thought to myself.

"What has you over there so stuck?" Sho-V asked as he threw me a beer and turned on the news. We were waiting for the police to release a statement about the car that was found. We wanted to be near each other when we talked to Qyleek and acted just as surprised as he did about Zay's car turning up in the woods.

"Nothing," I replied to him while standing up to go on the patio. There were about ten transactions like this, small increments of money that had been taken from different accounts. There was only one account that nothing had been taken from as of yet. I called Winsler Financial immediately to tell them to put a freeze on my account and notify me if anyone tried to come inside and pull money from the account. I then reached out to one of my young niggas and sent him Cami's location. I gave explicit instructions to follow the Audi, and as soon as she stopped at her next destination, He was instructed to use cans of spray paint to write *SLUT* all over her car. I cash apped him five hundred dollars, and ended the call.

Walking back inside of Sho-V's house, I stopped in the kitchen to grab a wing from the platter he had catered for us. A part of me wanted to open up to him and tell him what had been going on with Cami and me. I wanted to share with him what she'd done, as well as what I'd caught her doing the other day, but I didn't want to hear I told you so. We were going through something right now, but I still loved Cami. A nigga couldn't deny his feelings for her. I wanted to give her the chance to come to me and tell me what was going on so that we could fix it. If I told Sho-

V what she'd been doing, he would write her off as just another nothing hoe like he'd done Glow and Raleigh. I couldn't speak for those other two, but I knew Cami loved me, and she was a good woman. Even though she'd taken around ten bands from me, my heart told me that there was a good reason for it.

"Aye nigga, it's on! They found the truck, bring your ass!" Sho-V yelled, causing me to drop the wing and run into the other room.

"Local Police received an anonymous tip from campers that discovered a 2022 Cadillac Truck in some woods near a popular camp site. DMV records have revealed that the truck belongs to twenty-six-year-old Xavier Walters. Walters is one out of four owners of the popular cannabis dispensary, Weed Hut. He was reported missing a month ago," the news anchor concluded her report.

"Make the call nigga," I told ShoV as he picked up his phone to dial Qyleek's number.

"Hello," he answered.

"OH MY GOD, HAVE YOU HEARD ABOUT ZAY?!" Sho-V yelled loudly, putting on an Oscar-worthy performance.

"No. What about him? Where is he?" Qy asked back to back. I could hear the nervousness in his voice.

"The police just found his car by a camp site, my nigga. The camp site right under Dead Man's Curve," Sho-V told him while shaking his head.

"I'm about to head out there right now." Qy sounded like the wind had been knocked from him.

"They won't let you pass the yellow tape. Me and Bak just tried to get past to see what was going on, and they wouldn't let us," Sho-V lied.

"What's up, Qy? I just can't believe this shit, man. It's been weeks and the fuckin' pigs just gave up looking for my nigga," I joined in, faking heartbreak.

"Let me call his mother; they have to let us through. I will be in touch because they have me fucked up," Qy replied as his voice shook like he was trying to hold back tears.

I could understand how he felt. If something had happened to Sho-V's troublesome ass, I would've probably reacted the same way.

When the call ended, Sho-V turned to me."Do you think he believed it?" he asked.

"At this point, it doesn't even matter. He can stop stressing about it and finally get the closure he needs." I replied nonchalantly.

"I don't need the extra shit on my plate. If Qy wants to take over his stores and keep the profit, that's fine with me," Sho-V shook his head.

Before I could reply, my phone rang.

Answering it, a woman greeted me.

"Good afternoon, Mr. Bakari. This is a teller from Winsler Financial. Is it ok to discuss financial matters over the phone with you at this time?" she asked.

"Sure, it is," I replied.

"Well, you called us not too long ago and asked someone from the bank to notify you if someone tried to come and take money from the account you froze. Well, a young lady just left, angry, after she tried to do a ten thousand dollar withdrawal, and the account was frozen. I told her that I could call you to come down and unfreeze the account, and she insisted that she didn't want to. Are you currently a victim of identity theft?" the teller asked.

"No, I'm not. Was the young lady short, of mixed descent, with long, red hair and probably had a little boy with her?" I asked.

"Yes, she was. She's listed as an authorized user on the account, but when the account is frozen, no one has access —

not even if they're authorized. The only person that can make decisions for the account is the owner of said account," the teller informed me.

"Yes, I'm aware of your policy. You did the right thing, and thank you for contacting me," I told her.

There was nothing else we could do at the moment with this Zay situation but let the cards fall how they were supposed to. It was time for me to go home and have a conversation with my fiancée about what the fuck she had going on. Slapping hands with Sho-V, I left his house and headed home.

When I made it to the house forty minutes later, the first thing I noticed was Cami's car. My young nigga had overstood what was required. Her once beautiful baby was fucked up, and she would need an entirely new paint job. I know she was embarrassed riding around in her car like that all day. I laughed to myself, because that was what her ass deserved for being sneaky.

Walking up the stairs, I placed the key in the front door, and the smell of cookies hit me.

She and Prince had been baking, and it smelled like every flavor cookie combined. Prince laughed loudly, and I walked over to him.

"What's up, son?" I questioned.

"Hey, dad," he replied while laughing at the movie.

"It smells good in here. What have you and mom been doing all day?" I questioned.

"We ran some errands, went to pay some bills, which was boring. Ma took me to the park and I met—" he started before stopping with a guilty look on his face. He looked like he'd said too much, and I sat down next to him.

"You met who?" I asked.

"You know you can tell daddy anything, and mama doesn't have to know. Some things are just between us boys," I coaxed. He smiled at me and finished his sentence. "I met this creepy looking guy. He shook my hand and asked, "who taught you how to shake hands?" I told him my daddy. Then, him and mama sat on the bench while I swung, and she looked sad," he finished his story.

"Did the man make mommy sad?" I asked Prince.

He shook his head yes then turned his head back to the television.

I was furious. The only person that Cami could've taken Prince around was Sean. My plan of sending the message to him had backfired on my ass. I wondered if she'd been fucking with him.

"Cam!" I yelled out angrily as I walked through the house. I needed answers, and I was getting them tonight, no sneaky shit. There was no response as I walked through the house calling Cam's name.

"CAMI!" I yelled out, and I still received no answer. When I made it to our bedroom door, it was closed.

Turning the knob, I walked inside of the room, and I could hear water running coming from the bathroom. The door to the master bathroom was closed. She was probably in the tub washing her pussy because she'd been fucking Sean all day. Maybe she was even giving this nigga my money.

"CAMI!" I yelled angrily as I walked into the bathroom, busting the door open. When I opened the door, Cami was swinging back and forth from the upper railing above the bath tub. The water in the tub ran freely because the tub hadn't been stopped up. I raced to her and tried to snatch her body from the railing. She'd tied the rope really tight and it wasn't budging.

"Cami baby, you have got to be kidding me. Wake up, Cami!" I talked to her as I tried to saw through the rope with a pocket knife and a lot of pulling. Eventually, the rope snapped, and we both fell inside of the tub. Removing her body from the tub, I laid her on the floor and tried to perform CPR with one hand. With my other hand, I dialed 911 from my cell phone.

"HELLO OPERATOR, MY WIFE IS PREGNANT! SHE HUNG HERSELF, AND I'M TRYING TO GIVE HER CPR. SEND AN AMBULANCE TO 1518 TREEWELL COURT IMMEDIATELY!" I screamed out. When I looked up, Princeton was standing in the doorway. First, he looked at his mother. Then, he looked at me.

"Mama's alright, Prince; she's just sleeping," I told him as tears filled my eyes. Seeing some shit like this as a child would traumatize him for the rest of his life. If he lost his mother, he would never be the same again.

"Go into the front room for me. Some people are on the way to help your mom. I need you to be a big boy and let them in," I told him as I continued to do chest compressions on Cami like I had seen done before on TV. I'd never seen it done in real life or attempted it, but I knew I had to try.

"Why didn't you tell me, baby? What did he do to you?" I asked as I opened her mouth to blow air through it. I checked the side of her neck, and her pulse was barely there, but she had one. She wasn't dead yet. I removed the rope from her neck and moved her hair from her face, then continued to pump her chest until the medics arrived.

When they finally came to pick her up, I repeated to them to be gentle because she was pregnant. They strapped her to the gurney and rushed her to the nearest hospital. Reaching for my phone so I could follow the EMTs to the hospital in my car, I began to look for her phone as well, when I laid eyes on a stack of pictures laying in the tub. I was so transfixed by her hanging from the ceiling, I didn't notice that the water was running over a bunch of pictures that were soaking wet and sticking to the tub's surface. The pictures were of Cami in different pictures, getting fucked by the same nigga I'd reached out to. Princeton's birth father. When Princeton walked into the room, his eyes were red from crying. "Daddy, they're taking my mama." He reached out to me. He had the exact same face of the nigga who was on the pictures with

Cam. My heart was broken, but I scooped him up in my arms and held him tight.

"Mama is going to be alright. We're going down there with her so she won't be alone. I'm going to call grandma on the way. Go grab you book bag and put some clothes in it for me. Make sure you take your Nintendo DS, your charger, and some games. And pack some real clothes, underwear, and your toothbrush," I told him while walking him out of the bathroom and sitting him back on his feet.

"Ok." He nodded his head and ran to his bedroom. Going back into the bathroom, I grabbed all of the wet pictures out of the tub. I walked over to the closet and grabbed my 357 Magnum and placed it into my back pocket.

I found Cami's phone buzzing silently and walked over to put the code in it.

I expect you to be in my bed at the same time tonight. That fingering session in the park only got me started. You gotta finish me off tonight, the first message read.

The message immediately before that read,

Have the rest of my money in cash in three days, or hubby gets what I told you he's going to get. Oh, and go check the doorstep. I saw something on your porch for you.

I shook my head in disgust. Right under my nose, Sean had been fucking my bitch and blackmailing her to be quiet about it while she was pregnant with my seed.

An anger I'd never felt before consumed me.

Chapter Thirteen

Glow

When I opened my eyes, I'd never been this afraid in my life. I wasn't sure where I was. Was I still in the furniture store? Had I been moved somewhere else? Had Abdul kidnapped me? All I knew was what I could feel. I was sitting on a hard chair, my hands were bound behind my back, and my feet were bound tightly. There was something in my mouth stopping me from screaming, and my eyes were wide open, but I only saw darkness. There was something on my head that felt like a knapsack.

I couldn't believe I'd walked right into a trap. I'd fallen for the Arab man's kind smile and stupid "I dont know who you are" trick. Of course he knew who I was. Of course he knew that he was working in a drug trafficking furniture storefront. The scariest part about it all was that no one would come looking for me because no one knew where I was. I began to cry and pray in my head for some sort of miracle because that was the only way I was getting out of this situation. Trying to play detective had landed me here when I should have just focused my energy and efforts on Sho-V.

I heard talking in another language, and I immediately thought about that terrorist attack when the Taliban had chopped off that American's head on live television. Who knew what they were about to do to me. I wished I'd gotten the opportunity to hug my mother and tell her I love her one last time. The ironic thing was, as soon as I died, Sho-V would still win. They would pin the whole trafficking thing on me with no traces pointing back to him, and he would get away with everything.

Suddenly, the cloth was snatched from my face, and I had to blink hard and squint so that my eyes would adjust to the light. I looked around the room and noticed that it looked like we were in a dungeon. There was a single light swinging overhead, the floors were bare cement, and there were some boxes stacked up in the corner. From the looks of things, we could've possibly still been in the furniture store. After my eyes adjusted, I noticed Abdul as well as the fake sales rep standing in front of me.

"So, your boyfriend thinks he can play me and take my merchandise without paying?" he questioned while smiling at me.

I shook my head from side to side as hard as I could to let him know that I had nothing to do with what Ta'Shovi was doing.

The sales rep back handed me hard, causing the entire right side of my face to feel like it had been set on fire.

"Remove the gag from her mouth, Esmail!" Abdul instructed him as I tried my hardest to stop my head from spinning. That slap had damn near knocked me unconscious.

"Where is my money?" Abdul yelled at me loudly.

"I have no idea, Abdul. Ta'Shovi played me too. I didn't even know this was a drug pickup; I thought I was just furniture shopping!" I begged.

Before I could say another word, Esmail slapped me again. I think he was just enjoying putting his hands on me because I hadn't been uncooperative in any way.

"Why the hell did you do that?" Abdul questioned him.

"Clearly, she's lying," he replied in his thick, Arabian accent.

Abdul shook his head in annoyance.

"I was just released from jail yesterday. I haven't been in contact with anyone. Check my phone if you don't believe me."

"Enough of this shit. Let's make an example of her and send her head to her boyfriend." He pulled a gun from his back pocket, cocked it back, and pointed at my temple.

Tears streamed down my face, as I realized I was about to die. I thanked God that this would be quicker than the alternative. I would prefer a bullet to the head over being sex trafficked, raped, beaten, and tortured like the shit I saw kidnappers do in the movies. Maybe them chopping off my head would be all the revenge I needed to get on Shovi. For the rest of his life, the last image he would see before he closed his eyes would be my severed head. I would haunt him for the rest of his life, and that would be his karma for ruining my fucking life and introducing me to some shit I otherwise would've never been a part of.

I closed my eyes so that I didn't have to anticipate when it would happen, and suddenly, the phone rang.

"Who's calling your phone at this time?" Esmail asked him with broken English.

"I don't know. The number is unknown. Hold on for a second," Abdul told him, postponing my murder for a few more seconds.

"Speak," he answered his phone.

After a long silence, I opened my eyes to see if he was still standing there because all I could hear was Esmail's breathing.

Abdul stood, listening to the caller for a few seconds more before he told Esmail, "Come with me" and walked out of the room.

"Be right back." He smiled at me, pointed in the air, shot the bullet he'd put into the chamber, and put the cloth back over my head. I then heard his footsteps as he ran behind Abdul.

"God, help me," I prayed as I tried to pry my hands from the rope behind me. If I could free my hands, I could lean down and pull the rope from my ankles. I tried with all of my might to pull against the ropes, but they were bound too tight.

I tried to rock from side to side to see if I could tilt the chair. When I noticed the chair rocking, I leaned to one side, shifting all of my weight until the entire chair tilted over. I fell hard on my side, sending a shooting pain up the side of my body I'd fallen on. I wanted to sream out in pain, but I didn't want them to come and give me something else to knock me unconscious.

I wiggled around on the floor like a fish out of water for a few minutes until I heard a door open and loud footsteps heading in my direction. I went still and waited to see what would happen next.

"How did she end up on the floor?" Abdul asked with his heavy accent.

"I don't know; when I left, she was sitting upright," Esmail replied nonchalantly.

"Get her up and put her in the car; he's waiting for her," Abdul replied.

"Pleasure doing business with you!" Abdul yelled out in my direction, and my heart began to pound.

They'd gone and done exactly what I feared. They were giving me to someone else, who would probably do God knows what to me. I began to thrash wildly when Esmail put his hands on me to lift me up.

"Calm down before I give you some more sleepy potion," he laughed sadistically.

I struggled against him, trying my hardest to get out of his arms, until he pulled the gun from his pocket, and I felt the steel against the back of my head.

"Stay still, or I'll shoot you," he told me as he undid the ropes on my hands. Pulling my hands in front of me, I rubbed my wrist to get the circualtion flowing in them. I didn't make any sudden movements so his trigger happy ass wouldn't shoot me just because. He bent to work the ropes off my legs then grabbed me underneath my arm.

"Walk," he ordered, and I walked slowly with the cloth still on my head. When I heard the sounds of an alley, I could hear a car door opening, and I was forced inside.

"Thank you," I heard a voice say. This voice didn't have an accent and sounded vaguely familiar, but I was too afraid to focus on it.

"Same time next month," Esmail replied before I heard his footsteps walking away. I could tell that I was in the front seat of a car, and I was tempted to remove the cloth from my head, but I didn't want to make any sudden moves to upset my kidnappers.

When I heard the other car door open, the person get inside, and shut the door, I wrung my hands together nervously as the car cranked and pulled off. We rode in silence for a few seconds as I contemplated what to say, or if I should've said anything at all.

"If you don't take that shit off your head," I heard a familiar voice say, and I reached for the cloth and snatched it off quickly. I gasped in surprise as I came face to face with Zay.

"How was your day?" he questioned.

"WHERE THE HELL HAVE YOU BEEN?!" I screamed at him in surprise. I had never been so happy to see him in my life. He looked a little thinner, and he had scars on his face that looked like they were healing, but aside from that, he looked like the same old Zay I remembered.

"I've been here; we talk every night," he smiled at me.

"So that unknown number was you?" I asked him in surprise.

He nodded his head yes.

"The lawyer, the money on my books, the bitches leaving me alone in jail, the ten k in my account... it was all you, wasn't it?" I asked. He smiled.

Tears filled my eyes.

"I'm so sorry I didn't listen to you about Sho-V," I apologized.

It was my hard head that got me on this fucked up journey.

"If I would've steered clear of Sho like you warned," I started before he cut me off.

"It's cool, Glow. When I warned you about him, I was jealous. You were right to follow your own heart. Hell, I trusted him as well, and the nigga tried to have me knocked off," Zay told me as he pulled onto the expressway.

"He's fucking Qyleek's wife, and when I found out, I threatened to tell Qy if he followed through with pretending to like you so you'd drive the delivery truck," Zay told me.

"He agreed. The minute I left his sight, he put a hit out on me. My truck was shot up, and I flipped over Dead Man's Curve. I was in the woods for days until campers found me," he told me sadly.

My heart ached for him, and I felt terrible. Zay had damn near died trying to protect me, and while he was out suffering, I was stuck on Sho-V's ass, thinking I'd really found someone who loved me. In a way, I deserved everything that had happened to me for turning my back on the one person who'd always had my back, even long before Cami and I became friends.

"I'm sorry," I apologized to him again, as I grabbed his large hand and placed my hand inside of his. I owed him my life, and I would be forever indebted to him.

Chapter Fourteen

Bakari

When I finally made it to the hospital, I went to the nurses' station to find out what room Cami was in. A few seconds after I walked in, her mother rushed into the emergency room with an older man with her. She looked like she had ben crying, and I had never seen her so distraught.

"Grandma!" Prince ran up to her, and she held him tightly and kissed him feverishly all over his face.

"What happened to my daughter? Where is she?" she asked me urgently then turned to talk to the woman behind the desk.

"She's in emergency surgery. Please have a seat. The doctor will be out shortly," the nurse told her.

Her mother looked like she wanted to protest, but her guy friend rubbed her back to keep her calm.

"She sent me a text message that said, *take care of Prince*, but I didn't know what the hell it was about it," she told me, shaking her head as the tears began.

"It's ok, baby, she's ok; the doctors have her in the back, and she's going to be fine," he reassured her.

"I'm Bakari," I introduced myself to the man.

"Miles Davis." He reached out his hand to shake mine.

"I have heard so much about you, son. It's a shame we had to meet under these circumstances," Mr. Davis told me.

"How did you find her?" Cami's mother asked me.

"I found her in our bathroom. She was…" I was about to say *swinging from the railing*, before I looked down and noticed that Prince was looking up at me.

"Hey, big man. Want to go down to the cafeteria with me and see if they have any ice cream?" Mr. Davis asked Princeton.

"If mommy wakes up, I want her to see me," he protested.

"You will be the first face she sees when she wakes up. I promise," Miles told him while sticking out his pinky to do the pinky promise with Prince.

Prince stuck out his little pinky and linked it to Miles's. He then jumped from his chair and grabbed the man's hand.

When they were far enough away, I began again.

"I found her swinging from the upper railing in the bathroom," I told her mother solemnly.

"What has been going on? Has she been unhappy? Have you and her been having problems?" she questioned.

"I'm just as blindsided as you are. I thought she was happy with me. I handle the household, treat her like a queen, and give her everything she asks of me. I don't know what more I could do to make her happy," I told her mother sadly as I thought about the pictures of her with Sean. I would never look at her the same, and I prayed, for her sake, that my child was ok.

An hour later, the doctor came out of the room and delivered the bad news. They had saved Cami's life, but they were unable to save my unborn child, even after doing an emergency Cesarean. The baby had died from the trauma that her little lungs had gone through when she struggled to breathe. It was a girl.

The doctor cleared Cami to have visitors, and I told her mother that she and Princeton could go in and see her because I had something important to handle. Sending Sean's address from Cami's phone to mine, I gave her mother her phone and headed out.

The entire car ride over, I thought of ways to torture Sean for killing my little girl. I could chop his body up, part by part, while he was still alive so he could suffer in excruciating pain. I could drown him so he could know the feeling of not being able to breathe like my daughter did. The more creative ways I thought to torture him, the more I felt that Cami deserved the same fate as him. Sure, he had blackmailed her and caused her to attempt to take her own life, which resulted in my child dying, but it was still more of her fault than his. She had fucked him, sucked his dick, gave him my money, and even tried to kill herself. She had done literally everything besides come to me about the issue. If she would've come to me when she first started having issues with the nigga, I would've handled it, and my daughter would still be alive.

When I whipped into Sean's driveway in Cami's car, I was speechless at how huge his house was. The nigga clearly had bank — too much money to blackmail a woman into fucking him.

I pulled the hood over my head and used my gloved hand to turn the knob. The door was open, just like he told her it would be in the text message.

"Hey, sexy bitch. Tonight, I want to fuck you in my jacuzzi tub to see how that pussy feels in water," Sean said as he poured a glass of bourbon in a glass with his back turned.

I walked up to him slowly and put the gun to the back of his head.

"What the fuck?" he questioned while turning slightly.

"It's Bakari, nigga. Cami tried to kill herself tonight because of the sick shit you and her have going on. She survived. My daughter didn't," I told him.

Before he could say another word, I pulled the trigger, shooting him in the back of the head. I then emptied the rest of the clip, filling his body with bullets. I pulled the blanket from his bed, wrapped him in it, and found his car keys. Walking out of the mansion with his body wrapped in the blanket, I tossed it over my shoulder, making sure to keep my head down, in case he had any cameras. I threw his body into the trunk of his car and pulled it into the garage of an abandoned house nearby. When I was finished, I went back to Cami's car and dropped it off at the chop shop.

When I made it home, a part of me wanted to call the hospital to check and see how Cami was doing. The other part of me didn't give a fuck how she felt. I smoked a fatty and took a shot for my dead daughter, who I'd never gotten the chance to meet.

The very next day, I woke up early and headed to the hospital. Half of me wanted to hear what Cami had to say; the other half of me wanted to wring her lying ass neck. I wasn't sure which half would take control when I laid eyes on her. For her sake, I hoped it was the understanding half. I walked to the front desk and gave the receptionist her name.

"Fifth floor, room 518," the nurse told me politely while handing me a visitor's badge. I placed the badge on my shirt, and headed towards the elevators.

When I made it outside of her door, I stood for a few seconds, contemplating if I wanted to go inside. Concluding that I had come too far to turn back now, I grabbed the handle and stepped inside. An old episode of *Martin* played, and Cami laughed at the joke just as I rounded the corner and looked at her.

She lay in the large bed in a hospital gown. Her neck was bruised purple because of her light complexion, her long red hair was a matted mess, and she looked weak and small. When she laid eyes on me, her smile left, and tears filled her eyes.

"Hey," she murmured softly.

Unable to speak to her, I didn't reply.

She looked down and began to fidget with her gown, like she could make it look any better than it did. She was trying to keep herself busy too avoid my gaze.

I walked over to the seat near her bed and sat in the chair. I had all the time in the world to hear what type of excuse she was going to come up with for killing my child then cheating on me. I'd killed niggas for less.

"I'm sorry," she began.

"I love you and I never meant for any of this shit to happen," she finished while still avoiding eye contact.

"That's all I get? I've been taking care of your ass for two years. I provide anything you want and need. I bust my ass to make you happy. You go out and fuck your baby daddy, steal money from me to give it to him when he starts blackmailing you for being a hoe, and then you kill my flesh and blood just to avoid looking me in my face afterwards. The best you can give me is, you "never meant for any of this to happen"?" I questioned her while staring a hole through the side of her face.

"I know you're mad, Bak. But it wasn't on me. This nigga tricked me into fucking around with him then used it against me. Everything I did, I did because I love you," she replied.

I laughed in her face.

"Mad would be if you forgot to put the alarm on in the house. Bitch, you killed my daughter. I passed mad a long time ago!" I jumped up from the seat and walked closer to her face. It was taking everything inside of me to not punch her in her lying ass face.

"You stole ten thousand dollars from me. How do I know he was blackmailing you? You and him could've been plotting to steal from me from the beginning. Maybe all of the pictures and messages were a part of the plan to make it seem like you had no choice." I grabbed her by her hair and turned her face towards mine. She'd been avoiding eye contact with me the whole conversation, but I was done with her shit. I wanted her to look at me so she could see how deeply she'd hurt a nigga who would've gone through heaven and hell for her.

"Bak, that hurts," she complained as tears slid down her cheeks.

Gaining control of my emotions, I let her go.

"I didn't want to come to you because I didn't want you to react the way you're acting now!" she exclaimed.

"And you feel like the way you handled it was better?" I questioned.

"I thought if I gave in to his demands, he would go away. He already ruined my friendship with Glow. Popped up there out of nowhere, blowing a bitch cover and shit. To this day, I still don't know how the hell he knew where we were. He swears I sent him a message, telling him to come and meet me, but I didn't send no dumb ass message like that," she argued.

I laughed out loud, causing her to look at me weirdly.

Reality dawned on her as she realized why I was laughing. "You sent that message, didn't you? You sent that message because you knew that it would ruin our friendship. Why the fuck did you do that?!" she yelled at me angrily.

"That bitch wasn't your friend. I did you a favor," I dismissed her.

"She was the only person I had."

"She sucked my dick," I told her nonchalantly.

I smiled as I walked closer to her and whispered in her ear. "Yep, your best friend sucked my dick. She's a good for nothing bitch just like you are. You want to fuck around with your baby daddy, I'm going to send you where I sent him. Y'all will be together forever."

"What did you do to Sean?" she asked me fearfully as her eyes went wide with terror. I smiled at her and kissed the side of her face. The kiss was more out of hate than love. It was definitely a threat. The minute she stepped out of this hospital room, I was going to end her life. She was living on borrowed time, and she knew it.

"Bak, please, I love you. I made a mistake, and I know I was wrong. You don't have to do this. I have a son!" she called out as I walked away from her bed and towards the door. It was her last attempt to get me to spare her life.

"I had a daughter; you didn't spare her. Why should I spare you?" I yelled back over my shoulder before closing the door behind me.

Chapter Fourteen

Ta'Shovi

"Yeah, suck that shit," I coached Raleigh as she swallowed my dick and massaged my balls simultaneously. I could hear the loud sounds of her slurping and gagging while I held her head. We were sitting outside of her house in my car, and I was expecting her husband to pull up any minute. We didn't have time to fuck, but with the throat she possessed, she could make me cum in less than five minutes.

"I'm cumminnnn'" I grunted as I shot my baby gravy down her throat, and she caught every drop. Wiping her mouth, she jumped out of the car quickly and ran back into the house. Ten minutes later, Qyleek was pulling into the driveway.

After I called him and told him that Zay's car was on the news, he called me back a few hours later and asked if I could meet him at his house. Assuming he wanted to tell me about what the police concluded in Zay's investigation, I quickly called Bakari to tell him to come along as well. He didn't answer for me, so I decided to give him his space. Our business was running smoothly, so the only thing he could be stressed about was the bitch he proposed to. He didn't have to tell me he was going through it; he'd been my boy all my life. I knew when something was wrong just by the way he looked.

After getting invited to Qyleek's house, I swung by the barbershop for a shape up and went out to grab a new cologne fragrance to drive my mistress wild. I looked forward to sneaking glances at her fine ass. It would be worth faking sadness while Qy shed a tear or two behind Zay's death. I was just glad he had the closure he needed, and he could finally stop playing investigator and using all of his frequent flyer miles to fly all over the world, looking for a dead man.

When Qyleek pulled into the driveway and stepped from his car, I killed my engine and did the same. Jumping out of the car, I walked up to him with my arm outstrectched so that we could embrace the way we usually did. He hit my hand and pulled me into a tight, one-armed hug. When he let go, I could see that his eyes were red. He was either extremely high, or he had been shedding more than a few tears.

"Did they let you see him? Was he ok?" I questioned, faking concern.

"The car was so badly damaged. They found remains, and they have to test them," he replied sadly. "To think I've been flying here and there when Zay has been right here in Philly the whole time," he shook his head.

"You didn't do anything wrong, man. If we could leave the stores, Bakari and I would've been right along with you looking. Whatever his mom needs from me or Bakari, or anything she needs us to do for his funeral arrangements, we'll help with no problem," I told him as I put my hands in my pockets. "Thank God he didn't have a wife and kids waiting for him. Zay was like a brother to us, man," I finished while looking down to avoid eye contact with Qy.

"I know he was, and he could have had a wife and kids if he wasn't too busy chasing behind Cami's friend. He was obsessed with her ass, and she never gave him a second thought," he replied.

The fresh night air felt amazing, and the mention of Glow's name was threatening to take the high I was still riding on from the orgasmic release Raleigh had just blessed me with.

"He could do so much better," I dismissed Qyleek's

statement.

"I agree. Have you heard anything from Bakari? I tried to reach him, but he didn't answer. I called you both over here so we could discuss what to do with Zay's stores. I guess since tomorrow is Thursday, we can all get together and discuss it then," Zay changed the subject.

"I haven't heard from him since earlier, actually. He's been having some problems with Cami, so he's been a little distant. He proposed to her the other day because she's pregnant with his child, and I feel like he's starting to regret that decision. You know me, though; I'm always available. Besides the stores, what else is on your mind?" I asked him nonchalantly, hoping to get him to open up about Raleigh's cheating. He hadn't mentioned anything else about it since our last meeting when he downed an entire bottle of liquor. Being his friend had advantages. I could find out exactly what he knew about Raleigh's affair without looking suspicious.

"That was a misunderstanding; we had a long talk, and I realized I was just tripping. When you have a bad bitch like Raleigh, you're always afraid to lose her. That was just my own insecurity fucking with my head," he waved his hand dismissively at me.

"On another note, I know you deal directly with the plug. I was wondering if he's reached out to you regarding the product we have to pay for," he asked me.

Happy that he was off m and his wife's trail and he'd also let the Zay shit go, I began to smile. Everything was back to normal, and the plan had gone off without me having to set another nigga up to take the fall for the affair, like Bakari and I discussed. Whatever Raleigh had told him, had worked perfectly.

"I actually haven't reached out to Abdul. I haven't heard from him either. I'll hit him up as soon as I leave here," I assured Qyleek. While we were all partners, I was the only person who dealt with the plug directly. The heads of criminal organizations were picky about who they consulted with. They didn't usually want to deal with a lot of people. After the initial meeting with all four of us, we decided that he would only have one point of contact for supplying us product for the Weed Hut to make Abdul comfortable. My business partners and I decided that it would be best if I was the one who dealt with Abdul directly. Bakari, Qyleek, and Zay paid me the expected percentage from their stores, and I paid the plug while also setting up the way we received the merchandise. I also received the biggest profit.

"Cool, get with Abdul, and we'll discuss how we're going to move forward tomorrow at the meeting. Hopefully, we can get ahold of Bakari."

"I don't give a damn if I have to pull up to his spot and drag the nigga to JJ's Soul Food. This is business, and he can sulk about his Cami problems after the meeting is over," I laughed.

"You wouldn't understand what it's like becasue you don't let women get close to you, but I feel the brother's pain," Qy retorted.

"Well, I'm hungry as hell, so let me catch one of these restaurants before it closes," I told him while sticking out my hand to hit his hand. I had hoped to be around Raleigh a few minutes longer so she could see my designer drip and smell the cologne I wore for her, but our stolen moment was good enough for me.

"Fast food is going to be the death of you. Do you want to come in for dinner? The wife made a casserole," he offered.

"As a matter of fact, I haven't eaten shit all day. I'll take you up on that offer," I replied happily while following behind him into the house. He laughed and walked ahead of me while opening the door. When we stepped inside, the smell of food invaded my nostrils, and my stomach began to growl.

"Hey, husband, who I love. It took you long enough to get home," Raleigh greeted Qyleek as she stepped into the foyer. When she laid eyes on me coming inside behind him, her eyes shifted slightly.

"Hey.. Heyyyyyy, Sho-V. I didn't know we were having company tonight, baby," Raleigh stuttered, turning back towards Qy.

"We had to discuss some business, and the nigga was hungry. All he eats is fast food; he needs a home cooked meal," Qy joked.

Before she could open her mouth to respond, "Daddy's home!" his twins shouted, running to the door excitedly. Each son grabbed one of his legs, and he began walking and pretending to be a monster. He was so busy playing with the boys and walking further into the house, he had taken his attention from me and Raleigh. The last one at the door, I locked it behind myself and waited until Qy made it further in the house before slapping Raleigh on the ass. She turned to me and giggled softly.

"That's enough, boys. Let your daddy freshen up so we can eat!" she yelled out to her sons. When we stepped into the living room, Qyleek was on the floor. He wrestled with the boys as they tried to double team their giant father. I smiled as I watched them play and roll around. The love he had for his children was undeniable. I couldn't help but to reflect on my own father. Tajji Reynolds had been so busy chasing skirts all of my life, he'd never had time for me, my older brother, or my little sister. To deal with the pain of having a husband with a loose dick, my mother threw herself into her work. She was one of those mothers who believed that having both parents in the home, reflected positively on the children, even if both parents were unhappy.

The result of their marriage was an older brother who went to the military to escape the toxic environment, a middle son who lacked respect for women, and a daughter who grew up to be fiercly independent while emasculating men, especially her husband.

We were born with a silver spoon and had the best of everything, but we were a seriously screwed up bunch. To this day, even though my mother was dead, my father and I still didn't have a relationship. Maybe it was because I'd grown up to be just like him.

"Listen to your mother," Qyleek called out to his twins, bringing me back to the present. Father, sons, and their mother all laughed joyously. From the outside looking in, it looked like they had the perfect little family.

"Go get cleaned up and be at the dinner table in five minutes," Raleigh instructed them.

"I need to get cleaned up as well. I'll be right back," Qyleek told her while kissing her on the cheek and heading up the stairwell.

"Make yourself at home brother; what's mine is yours. Pour up a drink. You're standing over there, acting like a stranger," Qyleek joked with me as he walked up the stairs.

"I'll do just that," I smirked while following his fine ass wife to the kitchen. When she made it inside, I pulled her to me and kissed her passionately. Her breath tasted like toothpaste and mouthwash. She'd come inside and brushed her teeth to get the smell of my dick off her tongue.

My dick grew hard as I kissed her, and I wished I could bend her over the sink and fuck her roughly right next to the food she'd prepared for her husband and kids. Gaining control of myself, I pulled away from her and walked into the living room to pour myself a drink.

Ten minutes later, we were all sitting around the large dinner table, breaking bread. Raleigh had cooked a feast large enough for an entire village. The broccoli and chicken casserole, baked dinner rolls, green peas, and homemade apple pie for dessert smelled heavenly and definitely beat the fast food I would've been eating if I were home alone.

"How was your day, baby?" she asked Qyleek casually as she passed him the peas.

"I've had better days. The situation with Zay has been on my mind heavy since they found his car. I've flown to Dubai, New York, haven't gotten a good night's sleep in weeks, wondering where he was, just for him to be right in my own backyard," Qy replied sadly.

"Not at the dinner table in front of the kids," she reprimanded while giving him a look of warning. The twins stared at him silently.

"I'm sorry, kids, I'm sorry Queen. You're right. That isn't casual dinner conversation," he apologized to his family while looking at each one of them as he addressed them. That was something else I had never saw my father do. No matter how much he wronged my mother, my siblings, or me; he never apologized for shit.

"I can't lie; it's been on my mind as well," I lied.

"But, we will get through this together, like we've gotten through everything else together," I looked at Qyleek sternly.

"That's why your uncle Ta'Shovi is my brother, boys. He always has your daddy's back. When you get older, I expect y'all to have each other's backs the same way, you understand?" He looked at the twins. They nodded their heads hard, looking like a mirror image of each other. They were identical, and even though I had been around them all their lives, I even had trouble telling them apart.

"Your uncle Sho-V may have terrible taste in cologne — he has me about to choke with this new fragrance he's trying out — but I'm going to stick beside him," Qyleek cracked on me, causing the boys and Raleigh to laugh hard.

"Don't hate bro. This is that new Versace for men. I wish you would sit down that old school Cool Water you still use," I cracked back on him, causing the entire table to erupt in laughter.

"Well, I like your cologne, bro. It's a unique scent, and it definitely lingers. You can tell it's not cheap," Raleigh complimented. "Thanks, sis, I wish your husband wasn't such a hater," I replied.

"She's just being nice. I could smell your ass before I saw you," Qyleek cracked on me again.

"Whatever," I laughed as I placed a spoonful of casserole in my mouth.

"Now, on to lighter topics, what have you boys been up to all day?" Qyleek turned to his sons, smiling. They began to light up and tell their father all of the fun things they'd been doing all day.

After good food, laughter, and great conversation, I thanked Qy and Raleigh for having me for dinner and headed to my place on the other side of town.

Remembering to make the call to Abdul, my hand shook nervously as I prayed that he would be understanding about the situation. We would definitely pay him for the weed, but we needed to grab another shipment, or we'd be operating at a deficit.

The phone rang loudly in my ear, then his voice filled my car because my cell was connected to the Bluetooth that played over the speaker.

"Hello."

"Hey, my man Abdul, how have you been?" I asked, testing his temperature.

"Great man and yourself?" he asked.

"I'm ok, I've had better days, man. So, as you know, we had a hang up with the last shipment," I began nervously.

"I'm aware of that," he answered curtly.

"Well, I would like for us to settle the debt in a few weeks, if that would be ok because we really need another shipment. The supplies in the store are running low and —"

"Your debt has been settled. I will only discuss shipment details with one of you, and you are no longer the point of contact for this operation. Get with your partner, and he'll give you all the specifics." Abdul cut me off before ending the call in my face.

"Hello?" I questioned to make sure I wasn't tripping.

"Did he just say a one hundred thousand dollar debt has been paid already by somebody else in the group?" I asked myself aloud.

I immediately reached out to Bakari to see if he'd gone behind my back and paid the plug while appointing himself the new point of contact. I was angry as hell. I was making twenty thousand dollars more than my three friends because of the deal I'd set up. They were paying me more than I was paying for the merchandise, and they didn't need to know that. Whoever had taken my place would know it now and potentially tell the others. One of these backstabbing niggas had stabbed me in the back and took my position.

"Yeah," Bakari answered the phone dryly.

"Have you been talking to Abdul, nigga? Did you pay him what we owe without consulting me first? Are you the new point of contact?" I questioned him without ceasing as I switched in and out of lanes on the expressway.

"Hell no, nigga, Cami tried to kill herself. She survived, but she killed my daughter behind some sneaky shit she didn't want me to find out about. I haven't been talking to or worried about no damn plug. My stores are running smoothly, and my paper is good. I haven't stepped foot into Weed Hut, and I'm not dealing with anything concerning the business," he retorted.

He sounded broken, and I felt for him.

"I told you not to trust her ass!" I yelled at him loudly.

"I can't take an *I told you so* right now, nigga. See you at the meeting tomorrow, same time," he told me before hanging up in my face.

"These niggas are going to listen to me about these trifling, scandalous hoes one day," I laughed aloud to myself as I dialed Qyleek's number. *He had to be the one to have gone behind my back*, I reasoned with myself.

It all made sense. That was the reason he'd invited me over to dinner — to butter me up. He had also invited Bakari because he wanted to tell us together that he'd paid the plug and taken my position.

I called his phone, and he didn't answer it.

"That's why I'm fucking your bitch, you stupid motherfucker," I mimicked Tupac on his famous diss song. Qyleek thought he could fuck with me about my paper. He would be six feet under just like bitch ass Zay. These niggas had the right plan, but the wrong man.

When I made it home, I took a hot shower and jumped straight into bed. I would settle this shit tomorrow at the meeting. No one was going to take my paper or my spot.

Chapter Fifteen

Qyleek

"Dinner was amazing, baby," I complimented my wife when Sho-V left the house.

"Well, I'm sort of a chef, baby. What did you expect?" she laughed as she cleared the table and began to clean the kitchen.

"Let me help you with this stuff," I told her, standing from my seat and going around the table to help clear it.

"Thank you. I don't need your help, though. This is woman stuff; I've been doing it all my life. I know you're tired from being out all day. How about you head upstairs and get a hot shower and relax?" she replied to me sweetly.

I loved how my wife catered to me. She'd been raised old school and knew that the man was the king of the household. She had no problem with cooking, cleaning, taking care of the kids, and running the household while still maintaining her own business. She made sure me and the boys were always situated, and I respected her for that.

"I know you've been doing it all your life, but you cooked this big meal; the least I can do is help you clean," I retorted.

Shrugging her shoulders in surrender, she carried the plates in her hands to the kicthen. The boys had already been dismissed, and they were upstairs getting cleaned up to prepare for bed. It was just me and my sexy wife.

I grabbed the other bowls and plates from the table and

followed her into the kitchen.

"Baby, I wanted to apologize to you again for accusing you of messing around on me," I started as we cleared the dishes and placed the leftovers in plastic cartons so they could be frozen.

"It's ok, baby," she replied.

"No, it's not. I've been following up on this Zay thing and trying to keep everything afloat, running myself raggedy. It was my own insecurities that caused me to feel like you were stepping out," I apologized.

"I know, but when I agreed to be your wife, I agreed to rock with you for better or worse. You're a good man, and I would never hurt you," she replied while placing the last of the dishes into the dishwasher.

"I love how understanding you are," I told her as I put the frozen container down and walked up to her. Grabbing her by the side of her face, I began to kiss her passionately. She was so incredibly sexy to me.

Picking her up, I sat her on the counter and began to undo my pants as I kissed her on the neck.

Suddenly, my phone began to ring. She jumped and began to giggle nervously.

"You might want to get that, baby; it could be important if somebody is calling this late," she told me in concern.

I loved how she cared about me so much, she wanted to make sure I didn't miss anything important.

"Whoever it is can wait. It's our time now. You're my wife, and I've been putting everything before you," I murmered as I rubbed her thighs and eased my way up her dress. The more I kissed her, the more I began to smell a strange scent.

Ignoring it, I pulled her panties to the side and whipped my dick out. Stroking it in my hand, I tried my best to put it inside of her, but her pussy was incredibly dry. That wasn't like her. Maybe

I was being too eager because of how good she looked. I went back to kissing her all over her body as she moaned loudly.

No longer able to take it, I questioned the scent that was on her clothes.

"What the hell is that strong smell?" I asked her in annoyance.

She looked at me dumbfoundingly.

"I mean, are you saying my pussy stinks? I washed up," she defended herself.

"No. No, it's not your scent. It's another scent," I told her.

"Wait, Ta'Shovi did hug me good night. Maybe you're smelling that strong, stank ass cologne he just started wearing," she laughed loudly.

"That's exactly what it is. I need to make sure that nigga never hugs you again because he has your clothes lit up," I told her while spreading her legs and inserting my finger inside of her to see if she was finally ready to receive me.

"I don't want the kids to catch us. How about I put them to bed, and we can do it later?" she asked.

"I'm going to be quick," I assured her.

Sick of waiting, I spit into my hands and lathered her pussy with spit. I then stuck my dick inside of her and began to fuck her slowly. A few minutes later, I came hard as I busted a nut inside of her.

"That was good as hell, baby, did you cum?" I asked her while kissing her softly.

"Yes, baby, I came," she smiled at me sweetly while standing up and using a nearby napkin to wipe herself.

"I have to get a Plan B because you didn't pull out," she complained.

"Another baby wouldn't be so terrible." I rubbed her back

gently as I gazed at her with adoration. She was so beautiful, she made my heart skip a beat when I was around her.

"I don't want another baby. I'm satisfied with the twins," she shut me down before walking out of the room.

I dismissed her and went into the living room to have a drink of bourbon. Pulling my phone from my pocket, I looked at whose called I missed while I was digging inside of some good coochie.

I noticed I'd missed Ta'Shovi's call.

"That nigga probably just wants to thank me for dinner. I'll see him tomorrow at the meeting," I said aloud before going upstairs and taking a hot shower. I waited for Raleigh to come to bed, but it took her forever to finish up with the boys, and I could no longer hold my eyes open.

"She is such a good mother," I said aloud before the sandman took me to dream world.

The next morning, Raleigh snored softly beside me. I kissed her on the cheek before getting up to shower and get dressed. I had a lot of things that needed to be done today. Making a mental note, I reminded myself to go over to Xavier's house to clean it today. I had to find a good realtor to put it on the market, plan his funeral, and divide his stores. His mother was devastated, and she couldn't handle doing anything right now. I took a long, hot shower and cried silently as the hot water ran over my face and body. I couldn't believe my friend was dead. He had been a shoulder for me to cry on when I needed him the most. I would miss him dearly. The tears mixed with the watcr and washed down the drain.

After exiting the shower, I got dressed and cooked breakfast for the twins.

"When you finish eating, go turn on cartoons. Don't bother your mother; she's been under a lot of pressure, dealing with me and y'all two knuckleheads," I told my sons, as I kissed them both and gave them my love.

Leaving home, I headed towards JJ's Soul Food to meet Bakari and Ta'Shovi.

When I arrived, the restaurant was empty, which was new for them. They always had a full crowd. Going up to the door, I peeked inside to see if anyone was there and, one staff member was inside. Assuming the rest of the staff was in the back, I pulled the door handle to see if it would open, and it opened easily.

"Are you guys open to the public?" I asked the server, who was standing near the door.

"Are you here for the Weed Hut meeting?" she asked me nicely.

"Yes, I am," I replied.

"The event is a private event, and we've been paid to close the restaurant to the rest of the public," she smiled at me. "Follow me." She began to walk in the direction of our usual table in the back. Following behind her, I saw that Bakari and Ta'Shovi had already made it.

"What would you like for me to start you off with to drink?" the server asked when I sat down in my usual seat.

"Give us a second. We'll ring when we're ready," Sho-V cut me off mid-sentence.

"No problem," she replied before walking away briskly.

"What's the special occasion? Who bought the restaurant out?" I asked, turning to face Sho-V when I noticed he had a gun pulled on Bakari.

"What the fuck is going on?" I asked him angrily.

"Shut the fuck up," he replied as he pulled a gun out and pointed to me as well.

He sat with two guns pointed at each one of us. Bakari looked at him angrily but didn't say a word.

"Is somebody going to tell me what the fuck is going on? If a nigga is bold enough to pull a gun on me, he'd better be ready to use that shit," I threatened Sho-V.

"I'm always ready to send a nigga to meet his maker, you know that," he told me curtly.

"Ok, so that's settled. What is this about?" I asked him for the third time.

"I was hoping one of you could tell me. I called Abdul last night, and he told me that one of my partners paid him what we owed him and is the new point of contact. Zay is dead, so that leaves you two. Which one of you niggas is the backstabber that went behind my back and is trying to take my spot?" he asked, looking back and forth between Bakari and me.

"Nigga, I told you when you called me last night, I didn't do the shit," Bakari told him angrily while looking at him like he wanted to snatch his face off.

"Did you?" Sho-V turned towards me.

"Are you the new Head Nigga in Charge?" he asked me.

"I would never cross one of my brothers. If I would expect anyone to know that, it would be you. Loyalty is everything to me," I replied.

He had me fucked up if he thought I was going to beg him for my life like a little bitch. I'd just broken bread with this nigga eight hours ago, so if he felt that I could cross him, then he clearly wasn't my nigga, like I thought he was.

"You're the one who asked me if I'd spoken with Abdul. Maybe it was you, and you were going to use the little dinner last night to reveal it to both me and Bak. When Bak didn't come, it probably ruined your plans, so you decided to tell us today at the meeting," he told me.

"Nah, what I was going to tell you today at the meeting was Zay's mother is a mess. She wants to sell his house, and she needs us to go and get his affairs in order. It would've been pointless to tell you by yourself then repeat myself to Bakari later. I decided to wait until we could all sit down together and come up with a plan with how we're going to bury our brother," I replied solemnly as my eyes filled with tears.

I didn't need this shit right now. I was trying so hard to be strong and deal with the loss of my best friend to now have my other best friend accuse me of some shit I didn't do.

"Ok, both of you niggas are denying it. It's only one way to see who's lying. Bakari, call Abdul and put it on speaker phone," Shovi told Bakari while looking at him angrily.

Bakari shook his head in annoyance and whipped out his phone.

He then placed his phone on the table in clear view for us all to see. "Do you want me to go to the contact?" he asked sarcastically.

"Nigga, don't be funny. You could be calling the attendant from the seven Eleven. That could be anybody's phone number saved under that contact name. Oldest trick in the book. I'm going to give you the number to dial right now," he told him while calling the number out. As the phone rang, my heart thudded. I knew it had to have been Bakari because I knew for a fact that it wasn't me. We'd just lost one brother, and Sho was about to put a bullet in our other brother. What had once been a family, was falling apart in front of my eyes.

The phone rang twice before Abdul answered.

"Hello," he picked up.

"What's up, Abdul? How is it going?" Bakari greeted him.

"Great, man. Is there a reason you're calling me?" he asked suspiciously.

"Just calling to see when the next shipment will be," Bakari asked him while looking Sho-V in the eye.

"I don't discuss business with anyone that's not the point

of contact, like I told Ta'Shovi. Talk to your business partner and have him call me." Abdul ended the call in Bakari's face.

Giving Sho-V an *I told you so* look, he picked up his bourbon and swirled it around before taking a dramatic sip while still staring Bakari down.

"Too proud to apologize huh?" he asked Sho-V.

"My bad, twin," he retorted while turning both guns on me.

"Pull out your phone nigga," he told me.

"This shit is crazy," I told him angrily while pulling my phone from my pocket.

I placed the phone on the table in clear view, mimicking Bakari, and dialed the number as Sho-V called it out.

The phone rang once before Abdul answered it angrily.

"What is it?!" he yelled.

"Hey Abdul, it's been a minute, man. Just reaching out to see when we can expect the next shipment," I asked him casually.

"This has got to be some sort of joke, right? I feel disrespected, like you all are playing in my face," Abdul replied angrily with his thick accent.

"I don't understand—" I started before he cut me off.

"I ONLY SPEAK TO ONE PERSON. THOSE ARE THE RULES. GET THE FUCK OFF MY PHONE BEFORE YOU ALL HAVE TO FIND A NEW SUPPLIER!" he yelled at me before hanging up in my face.

Ta'Shovi looked at the phone in shock while still pointing the gun at me.

"Can you get that gun the fuck out of my face now?" I asked him angrily.

"My bad bro, I just don't understand." He scratched his head in confusion. How can neither one of us be his point of contact for a business only we own?"

"There's some fishy shit going on," Bakari replied.

"I'm going to figure out exactly what it is," Sho-V replied angrily.

"Good. Go and investigate. But the next time you point a gun at me, nigga, use it, or I'ma blow your fucking head off," I told him angrily. "Calling niggas to the table with guns drawn like one of those old gangster movies. You been watching *The Godfather*?" I asked as I laughed loudly.

"My bad, brother." Ta'Shovi laughed at me as Bakari burst into laughter as well.

"Nigga had this shit all mapped out," Bakari cracked on Sho-V as we laughed together.

"My bad. I told y'all niggas I apologize," he laughed as he placed his guns into his waistband.

"Can we eat? 'Cause I'm hungry as hell." I called the waitress over to place our order.

"This nigga went all out— shut the restaurant down, shades drawn, put on his most expensive cologne, and wore his good shoes to end a nigga's life," Bakari taunted Sho-V.

"Yeah, only the best to end one of my day ones," Ta'Shovi retorted, but the smile had been wiped from his face, and he and Bakari looked at each other coldly.

"Chill, y'all chill. We figured out that it was neither one of us. I agree with Sho-V. If you got bit by a snake, would you rather cut off your finger to save that hand or lose your life because you let the posion kill you?" I asked him.

"What the hell are you even talking about?" Ta'Shovi turned to me in confusion.

I took a deep breath before I began. "When you get bitten by a snake, especially one you don't see coming, the surprise of being bitten can make the venom spread quicker. The venom, not the bite, is what's deadly. If you can isolate the part that's infected, you can still save the rest of the body," I concluded.

"Thanks for the lesson on reptiles, Crocodile Dundee, but what does that have to do with my brother holding me at gun point and accusing me of something I told him I didnt do?" Bakari asked.

"Well, if he could isolate who was doing the snake shit and eliminate that person, the brotherhood can continue. The business we created together will continue. If we let disloyalty spread, it will be the venom that will kill off everything we built together," I explained.

"That makes perfect sense," Sho-V turned back to Bakari.

Nodding his head in aggreance, Bakari took a sip of his bourbon.

After ordering our food, we discussed how we were going to split the profits for Zay's stores, who would take which property, and also planned his funeral. What had started as a crazy meeting ended up great as we handled business, laughed, shared a meal, and reminisced on old times.

When we were finished eating, Sho-V took the tab.

"I'm full as shit," he stood from the table last. When he stepped into the aisle, I noticed the shoes that Bakari had spoken about earlier.

"Those motherfuckers HARRDDDDDD," I complimented as I looked down to further inspect Shovi's sneakers.

"Yeah, I know it." Sho-V modeled his foot and turned it around so I could see the detail of the shoe.

"These are the off-white MCA University Blues," he smiled proudly.

"I bought the last pair from online a few months ago. They cost three racks. It ain't a nigga in the city that got these. You know I'm *that* nigga," he boasted.

"Don't stand too close now, these are a collector's item. Don't be breathing on them. Putting your hot ass breath on my shit," he joked.

I laughed and pushed him playfully.

"I got a key to your crib, nigga. We wear the same size. They'll be in my house by the end of the month," I retorted as we stepped outside into the fresh air.

"Do I need to pull this gun back out on you?" he questioned, causing Bakari and me to double over in laughter.

"Do what you have to," I replied while walking to my car.

I was full as hell and headed to my store as I pulled out of the parking lot.

My phone suddenly rang. Answering it over my Bluetooth, a professional voice began to speak.

"Hi, Mr. Hudson. This is Amy Lexington from Crawford Long Hospital. Your grandfather, Marshall Hudson, was in a bad car accident. You're the only living relative he has. Can you come down to Atlanta to make decisions for his care?" the woman asked.

My heart began to speed up. Marshall was my mother's father and her last living relative. He was the reason she moved us from Atlanta to Philly. He had molested her all her life then turned her mother against her, causing my mother to take her only child and start over new in another city. I'd heard all about Marshall but never met him. I didn't want to meet him

My mouth wanted to say let his pedophile ass die, but my heart wouldn't allow me to. My mother would turn over in her grave, and my love for her outweighed my hate for him.

"I'll be on the next flight out," I told the woman after taking down her contact information.

I then called my wife to see if she was home. I needed her to pack me a bag so I could hop on a quick flight to Atlanta. I was honoring my mother by going, but if my grandfather was up and alert, I was going to give him a piece of my mind for what he'd done.

"Hey, husband."

"Hey, wife. Look, I have to take a flight to Atlanta to deal with some family business. Can you pack me a bag for two days? I looked up my flight, and the next one leaves in three hours. I can make it through security if I don't stop in the house and pack," I told her.

"No problem, I can do that. See you in a little while," she replied before ending the call.

"God, I love that woman," I said aloud as I drove to the house.

When I pulled in front of the door, she was standing outside with my bag packed, looking sexy as hell.

"You are too fine to belong to me. Whose wife are you?" I joked with her as I stepped from the car and grabbed my bag.

"All yours," she smiled at me and gave me a kiss.

"Do you need me to take you to the airport?" she asked.

"No, I didn't want you to round up the kids, so I ordered a rideshare. My Uber is right behind me," I told her.

"The kids are gone with my mother for the day," she replied.

"Cool, get some rest then. You deserve a kid free day. Go get your hair done, a mani, pedi, do some shopping. Treat yourself to a nice restaurant, and let someone cook for you for a change. I'll call you when I land at Hartsfield," I told her as the driver pulled into my driveway.

"I love you," I called over my shoulder.

"I love you too," she replied.

"Mr. Hudson, right?" the driver greeted me.

"That's me," I told him as I got into the backseat of the car.

The driver exited the driveway and headed in the direction of

Philadelphia International Airport.

Finally settled, I took a deep breath and reflected on the crazy day I'd had.

Forty minutes later, I received a text message from one of my store managers, asking if I was en route to bring her the store's expense report.

Shit! I forgot I was supposed to bring you that. Give me a quick second. I can email it to you

I texted her as I opened the bag that Raleigh packed to get my laptop.

"A boss's job is never done," I said aloud as I rummaged through all of the items in the bag.

Boxers, T-shirts, aftershave, tank tops, jeans, sneakers.

"Dammit, no laptop," I said aloud.

I will have it to you by the end of the day, I texted my manager.

"Can you turn around? My wife didn't pack my laptop?" I told the driver while going over to Raleigh's contact to call her so that she could bring my laptop outside.

"I'm sorry about this, young man. I'll pay you double the cost of the ride and tip generously," I told him nonchalantly.

"Thank you, sir. I appreciate that," the young boy replied happily.

Continuing to dial her number, the phone rang incessantly then went to voicemail.

Where the hell is she? I questioned as I settled into the ride. Hopefully, I could still make my flight on time.

When we pulled back up to my house, I noticed a Tesla in the driveway.

Ta'Shovi must have stopped by looking for me, I thought to myself. I tried to call the phone again, and Raleigh still didn't answer.

"Give me a quick second," I told the driver, as I stepped from the car and walked up to the door. Taking my key from my pocket, I opened the door and stepped inside of the house. I was immediately hit with Sho-V's loud cologne.

Shaking my head, I almost yelled out for him, until I stepped down on something soft.

"What the hell?" I looked down and noticed the dress Raleigh had just greeted me at the door wearing. The rest of her clothes were in a trail, leading up the stairs. My heart began to beat erratically.

When I made it to the bedroom door, the last item on the outside was a pair of low, off-white MCA University blue shoes.

"They'll be in my house by the end of the month," I'd joked with Ta'Shovi earlier as he bragged about being the only nigga in the city to own a pair.

I smiled as I turned and walked back down the stairs and out of the door.

Chapter Sixteen

Cami

"Thank you for all of your help," I told the nursing staff as I signed my release forms hurriedly.

They didn't want to release me, but I had the final say so. I had to get the fuck out of there before Bakari came back. I didn't have time to go to my mother's house to pick up Princeton, so he would have to stay with her. Bakari wouldn't hurt either of them; it was my head he wanted.

Pulling on pair of jeans, a T-shirt, and some sneakers that were donated to the hospital so women would have something to wear if they didn't have clothes, I jumped into the cab that was sitting outside of the hospital.

"Do you accept cash app?" I asked him as he pulled off.

"Yes, I do. Where are you headed?" the cabbie asked.

"The airport," I replied as I whipped out my cell phone and turned the power on. I had a few thousand saved in a private account that I could survive off of until I figured out what to do next. If I went back to our house, I had no doubt in my mind that Bakari would put a bullet in my brain.

Legend

"There's a phone call for you, Legend Turner." My assistant tapped on my office door as I looked through the files of the last case I had investigated.

"Who is it? I told you to hold my calls," I reprimanded her. As the head of the Federal Bureau of Investigations, I was always getting pulled in a million different directions. If I didn't set boundaries, the bureau would run me crazy.

"It's your Aunt Mina. She says it's urgent," she told me hurriedly.

Picking up the phone for my favorite aunt, the first thing I heard when I put the phone to my ear was her crying.

"What is it, Aunt Mina?" I asked fearfully.

"It's your cousin, Sean," she said as she cried too hard to finish her sentence.

WANT TO INTERACT WITH T'ANN MARIE & HER TEAM? JOIN OUR READERS GROUP ON FACEBOOK!

https://bit.ly/2TfYBL

WIN PRIZES, BE APART OF LIVE BOOK DISCUSSIONS & MORE!

Join Our Mailing List:

http://eepurl.com/gU81k5

TMP
TANN MARIE PRESENTS
is now accepting submissions in the following genres
URBAN FICTION * URBAN ROMANCE
STREET LIT * URBAN PARANORMAL
INTERRACIAL ROMANCE
for consideration, please email the first 5 chapters of your manuscript to:
TANNMARIESUBS@GMAIL.COM

www.ingramcontent.com/pod-product-compliance
Lightning Source LLC
Chambersburg PA
CBHW052017150726
47999CB00004B/1698